REDEMPTION

VINCENT AND EVE BOOK THREE

JESSICA RUBEN

JessicaRubenBooks, LLC

229 E. 85th Street

P.O. Box 1596

New York, New York 10028

Copyright c. 2018 Jessica Ruben

Paperback ISBN: 978-1-7321178-5-3

E-Book ISBN: 978-1-7321178-4-6

Printed in the United States of America

Contact me by visiting my website, JessicaRubenAuthor.com

Cover Art Design by Okay Creations

Editing by BilliJoy Carson at Editing Addict

Editing by Ellie at LoveNBooks

Publicity by Autumn at Wordsmith Publicity

❀ Created with Vellum

1

VINCENT

Beads of sweat trickle down my chest and onto my abs within mere moments of stepping onto the gray concrete. Squinting my eyes from the blaring sun, I crack my neck from side to side, letting out tension as my eyes take in the huge cement blocks around me.

Me and Tom, my best friend and brother in the Borignone mafia, are personally escorted off the prison grounds, our heavy strides silent against the dark pavement as we walk to our freedom. The warden and two highly armed officers flank our sides. A throat clears as a lone black Mercedes-Benz pulls up to the tall gates.

Tom turns to me, smirking like a beefed-up demon as his green eyes twinkle with triumph. Prison did nothing but make my boy tougher both inside and out. The guards step back. Tom swiftly opens the door, bending his thick neck low and entering the car.

I move to face the straight-backed warden, his bald head perspiring from the sun. He takes my hand in a firm shake.

"I won't forget what you did for me, sir. Thank you." I feel nothing short of honest gratitude. If not for the warden, I'd be leaving as nothing but an ex-con. Instead, I'm heading out of here as the board president of what will be one of the largest gaming companies in the USA.

"No doubt, son, you're one of the good ones. I hope to never see you again." He chuckles, his timber gravelly and strong as his hand continues to grip mine. I finally let go and step into the car, shutting the door firmly behind me. It closes with a satisfying *slam*.

I'm free, sort of.

It's been six years, five months, and fourteen days; my sentence lessened due to good behavior. And now I've got six months on parole before I can leave New York behind me—for good.

The driver starts down the dirt road wordlessly, his orders likely already given by my father Antonio Borignone, the boss of the Borignone mafia. Tom and I face away from each other, staring out our respective tinted windows. Boxy white mobile homes come into view as my eyes slightly water from the smell of fresh leather seats. It's that new car scent everyone loves but always bothered me with its sharpness.

Green trees enter my vision next, and the unexpected burst of color has my eyes widening. Prison is all grays and blacks, all the time. Absentmindedly, I rub the center of my chest as an acute feeling of worry seeps inside, blocking the relief I felt only moments before. What if a cop pulls us over and says there was an error with my paperwork during discharge? There are rumors that a misplaced signature can get a person back inside on the quick. I shake out my shoulders, telling my consciousness to shut the fuck up. It's not like me to double and triple guess myself like this, but what can I expect after being locked up for over half a decade? Freedom is here, yet I have this sinking feeling someone is going to take it away from me.

Being locked up is hell, although I know I deserved the punishment. I made wrong choices, which led me to ruin my world along with both Eve's and Tom's. I was an impulsive and hotheaded kid, believing I could have my girl in secret while publicly dating a socialite for the family. But this compartmentalized life brought me nothing but divide. Unable to get a good grip on the world around me, my life fell apart.

I've had years now to go over my mistakes, and now that I'm free, it's time I redeem myself. Once, being the son of Antonio Borignone defined me. But now I understand I'm my own man. What I do is on me, and me alone.

The low growl of motorcycles ring in my ears. I've got to get myself a ride. Considering the fact that I've spent years caged like an animal behind steel and metal bars, the idea of being free on the road without the restriction of a roof and doors sounds incredible.

The car begins to shake as a swarm of bikes surround us; my body and mind switch to alert mode; I look left to right, forward and back. Four motorcycles are on either side of the vehicle, plus two in front and two behind. They're wearing leather vests but moving too quickly for me to identify the insignia on the back.

One of the bikers pulls dangerously close to our car. He turns his head as a dark grin spreads across his face—raising a hand in what looks like...solidarity. My pulse quickens. I finally get a good look at his leather. This is the outside arm of the Boss Brotherhood, also known as the BB.

They're a group of white supremacist bikers with nothing but stupidity, muscles, and drugs between them. The fact that they work with the family is the tip of the iceberg when it comes to what I see as the degradation of the Borignone mafia. It's a downward spiral I'm not interested in taking part in—not anymore. And if I get my way, I won't have to any longer.

"Holy fuck, man. This is insane. Enemies inside, friends outside?" Tom's voice has a hard and confused edge.

We both knew the family aligned with the BB but still, seeing it in real time is a new thing entirely.

"Christ," I mumble, fantasizing about opening the window and grabbing the fucker's throat.

I clench my fists but lean back. "Sit, brother. We're not packing and I'm not getting us back inside within twenty minutes of leaving. They aren't showing aggression and we have no reason to fight."

"Fuck!" Tom slams his fist into the empty seat in front of him. He presses his lips together in a thin line, his tell for when he's calming himself. "You're right," he replies after a few beats, his voice resigned.

Finally, the bikes take off, leaving us unharmed.

Tom leans forward and touches the back of the seat in front of me, getting the driver's attention. "Stop at a restaurant, man. We're starved."

I nod. "Good call." The thought of food has my stomach grumbling.

Thirty minutes later, we pull up to what looks like a 1950s-style diner. The structure is low and white with two rows of pink neon lights highlighting the roof. I strut inside, the door chiming with our entry. It's strange walking into a restaurant as if I were just a typical law-abiding citizen when just an hour ago I had cuffs around my wrists. Yet, here I am.

Tom follows me to the back corner booth where two over-sized white menus are already placed on the table along with silverware and a red and white checkered napkin. I've got a good spot, able to watch the entire diner as well as keep an eye on the parking lot. Can never be too careful.

I sit down and scan the food choices, letting my eyes ping-pong between appetizers, main courses, and desserts. In prison, we had no choice when it came to food. Hell, we barely had a choice when it came to anything. I'm staring at over fifty potential meal items and the list seems endless.

Frustrated, I drop the menu back on the table, noticing an over-weight trucker sitting alone in the booth in front of ours. His red face shows a tired contentment as he digs into a huge slice of apple pie with a dull silver spoon. My mouth waters.

"We did it, huh?" Tom's voice brings my attention back to him. "There were moments, I swear to God, Vincent, I thought time would never pass," he admits.

"We were lucky though."

"True." He nods his buzzed head in agreement.

Our prison stay wasn't as difficult as it is for most inmates. For one thing, the skillsets we were raised on easily translated into prison culture: mental toughness, physical strength, and ability to lead. We also had a pre-existing structure within the system to plug into, as seven of our boys were already doing time.

The waitress steps over to take our orders, a pink apron tied around her short white uniform. She's young with bleached-blonde hair; I cringe remembering the girl who Eve believes I was with in our bedroom that fateful night. Goddamn, but the memory of watching her heart break in front of my eyes still burns.

Mouth widening in excitement, the waitress stares at Tom as if she just hit the jackpot. His eyes rove her body hungrily, like an animal starved. Not that I blame him. It's been a long time.

I clear my throat and the waitress turns to me. I order a double cheeseburger, fries, and Coke with extra ice. Apple pie, the same one as the guy in front of me, for dessert.

Instead of writing down my order, the girl's gaping at me, frozen to the spot. I look at her notepad, then her eyes, silently telling her to get her ass into gear. She swallows, pupils dilating, before finally jotting down my order. She's attracted but also scared.

"I'll have the same," Tom tells her with a crooked smile, causing her to erupt in a nervous giggle.

"Uh, I'll go get you guys your order." She stumbles her words before scuttling away with a bright red face. I shake my head at Tom.

"Not even a minute, huh?"

"I'm just glad to see I've still got it," he laughs. "I know what I'm doing tonight, and it isn't jacking off like I've been doing for almost seven years. The first thing I wanna do, after this meal of course, is fuck my brains out." He grabs the edge of the table and pitches forward to get closer to me. "You think the waitress would take a five-minute break to suck me off in the bathroom? After the burger?"

"Five minutes? I'd put you at thirty seconds."

He happily shrugs his shoulders. "What about you? I'm sure she'd do us both. Although you might be too much for her."

"Yeah, you're right, my ten-inch dick would definitely scare her." I quirk my mouth in a half smile and Tom laughs out loud.

"Man," he says, shaking his head from side to side. "She took one look at you and almost pissed herself. You got a bad case of resting murder face. As scary as you looked before—you're worse now." He laughs. "Those Indian black eyes of yours. Shiiiiit."

"*Native American*, you fuck head." I casually shrug at the dig, but he isn't wrong. I'm bigger and harder than ever. We both are.

"Not my type, anyway," I reply, leaning back in the booth and crossing my arms over my chest. It's been a while since I've sat without guards watching my every move and the independence is shockingly unnerving.

"I won't say that bitch's name, because it makes me sick what she did to us. But tell me you aren't still thinking about her after all these years."

I immediately sit up, gripping the edge of the table. "I may be leaving the life, but if I ever hear you talk about her like that again, I'll kill you. I told you before we were locked up, and I'll remind you again now that we're out. She didn't do shit. I made choices." I point at my chest with my thumb. "I did those wrongs. What happened to me and you is all. On. Me."

He leans closer. "Man, this is why you're supposed to be the Boss." His voice is a conspiring whisper. "It's in your blood. Don't walk away from it, Vincent. You take responsibility for yourself. We both know if the tables were turned, I woulda said the girl had me whipped. But you—"

"I love you like a brother, but I'm not on board with the new direction the family's rolling in." I shake my head slowly from side to side. "Just can't do it anymore."

"Your dad is gonna freak the fuck out. I mean..." he exhales. "Maybe you wanna wear a Kevlar before you have your chat?" It's spoken in jest, but I can tell Tom is worried. While we've discussed my plans about leaving the family for good, my father doesn't know about my decision yet.

Tom's chosen to stay inside the fold, unable to see anything in his future outside of the family. If anything, prison solidified his loyalty. Still, we've lived our lives side by side since we were born. Leaving prison together was a given—the family made sure of it. While we'd never admit it to each other, parting ways is unsettling. Still, it's just the way life goes. I know the conversation with my father won't be easy, but truth? I'd rather die than keep this shit up and I've spent years now coming to terms with it.

The waitress walks back to the table with large white plates of food. The moment I see the juicy burger sitting between a toasted sesame seed bun, every thought previously in my head disappears; I take a huge bite and groan. Neither of us speaks until our plates are completely clean. Dessert is more of the same; not so much as shifting until every crumb is transferred into our mouths and rinsed down with gigantic ice-cold sodas.

* * *

The car pulls up to Park Avenue and Seventy-Fifth Street.

"Wish it weren't this way, brother." Tom puts out his fist and I knock mine against his. He opens the door and steps out.

The driver continues uptown, taking me directly to my father's townhouse. My right leg bounces up and down as we swerve through city traffic.

"Sir, do you mind if I take First Avenue? My GPS is telling me there's an accident on Park."

"No problem," I reply, noticing the super high-tech screen planted on his dashboard. Goddamn, a lot changed while I was locked up.

The car turns east before taking a left on First. I squint my eyes in confusion, seeing designated bike lanes running up the street. The mayor must be insane to do this; I can only imagine the potential for accidents.

Turning west, we drive up Ninety-Second Street, pulling over between Madison and Park. I thank the driver politely as I open the door.

Stepping out of the car, I stand tall and inhale the city air. It isn't fresh or clean, but it's free.

My eyes examine the block as the clouds overhead cast a dull gray tinge on the row of brick and limestone townhouses. Three black SUVs sit idly, double-parked along the quiet tree-lined street.

Turning toward my father's townhouse, the home I grew up in, I count ten security cameras framing the mansion's entrance—five more than before I went into lockup. It still looks like an embassy opposed to a personal residence. I can just imagine him now, watching me like a hawk from the fifth-story window while he smokes cigarette after cigarette, stewing.

The car drives away and I feel a surge of heat rush over my body. With a rolling stomach, sweat breaks out on my forehead. I slick my short hair away from my face, feeling dampness at the roots. It must be stress. The combination of leaving lockup, entering this house, and the looming talk about leaving the family is giving me an emotional reaction. *Fuck*, I've got to get a grip.

I inhale through my mouth and exhale through my nose as I walk up the wide steps to the front door, imagining myself setting fire to this entire place and burning it to the ground. Still, I've got no choice but to deal with what's ahead. I move to ring the bell, but the door swings open before I make contact.

"Vincent." My father pulls me into the house before stepping into the doorway. His eyes scan the street. Seemingly satisfied there's no one watching, he moves back inside and shuts the door; the crystal chandelier hanging above our heads sways from the force. Gripping my shoulders, he apprises me. His hands dig into my biceps as if to incapacitate. I can easily get out of his grip. Yet, I stand still, not wanting to aggravate him. In the last few years, he's become increasingly more paranoid. I need to do my best to keep him calm, especially today. With a man like my father, the less I say, the better.

Finally, he lets me go.

"Come with me," his voice is stern, "lots to go over."

I don't reply. I was never much of a talker, but my solitary demeanor only increased with time and circumstances. With heavy steps, I follow him up the red-carpeted staircase.

I crack my knuckles, noticing the place hasn't changed at all, still showy and ornate like an Italian palace. We enter the white-marble kitchen on the second floor and my eyes zero in on the surface of the dining table, filled with files. "All for me?"

His electric-blue eyes shine; the idea that my casino and hotel complex is close to completion and all the money that'll be rolling in excites him to no end. Still, seeing all my hard work in front of me like this is straight-up astounding. It was dirty business getting the Tribal Council on board to partner with me, but when one of the older board members died, there was a perfect spot open for the taking. The family managed to pressure them to grant me a seat within a year of my going to prison—with less bloodshed than we initially thought. Once that bridge was crossed, I let the Council know of my intention to start a gaming operation. Luckily, with a few well-placed and heavy bribes, my current predicament of being in prison while creating a gaming operation was dropped into the basket of *sovereign immunity* under the Tribal Nation.

I studied everything about building and development. Internet access could have been an issue, but my attorney had it worked out that the warden himself would monitor my emails. With nothing to hide, having him look through my electronic correspondence was the least of my worries. Every single detail of this business had to be perfectly constructed—and it is. I won't allow ignorance of any law getting between me and my goals.

Negotiating with the builders and architects was difficult considering the circumstances, but I managed. People came to the prison weekly, and meetings were held on bolted-down plastic tables in the far corner of the cafeteria. Deals were brokered, and slowly, I built a team of trustworthy and hardworking professionals. Concurrently, my lawyers worked on my behalf to obtain all construction and building permits, approvals, and bank loans.

The Tribal Council came to me on the first Monday of every other month, flying across the country so we could work in tandem. It started out as an angry and awkward partnership due to the fact that Borignone muscle was used to force me at their table. But it didn't take long for them to realize I wasn't there to screw them over. I took my birthright seriously and expected the Milestone to advance and better the Tribe's day-to-day lives; I made sure the Council understood that.

As the work took shape, the parts within me that were disjointed pulled together. The creativity. The business acumen. All my studies in school. Street smarts. Negotiation. My days of fragmentation were over and I'm proud as hell of what I've accomplished.

Taking our respective seats across from each other, I stare at the light shining off the corner facets of the crystal and glass dining table. My mind wanders into an idea for the front desk in the main hotel's lobby.

My father shuffles in his chair. "I set up a work area in your bedroom; monitors with large screens have been outfitted."

"Tomorrow morning I'll move to my own place." No way in hell I'd stay here willingly. A few weeks ago, I had my lawyer set up a rental for me in midtown; the lease begins tomorrow.

"What's wrong with this fuckin' house?" His voice is aggressive as he stares me down.

I squint my eyes, taking note of his overly exaggerated response. "I just want my space." My voice is calm, meant to take the situation down a notch.

He hands me a file with hostility. I force my hands to steady as I open it. It's the descriptions and numbers for the gaming floors, which I spent years meticulously planning out: 5,000 slot machines, 250 table games, as well as a race book.

I clear my throat, switching my gear to work-mode. "Economically, we should be able to employ roughly seven thousand locals. I've done the math— we'll have about $1.03 billion in revenue per year. Concerts and boxing events will also bring in further employment and money."

"Excellent," his voice is enthusiastic. "I think the more locals we employ, the better the goodwill with the state."

"A lot of people will move here specifically for the casino and hotel management positions. I've been toying with the idea of subsidized housing for the employees who live off the rez. We have a great team in place, so building that out shouldn't be complicated."

He looks at me in annoyed confusion. "Why not just build out a few apartment complexes and let the workers rent directly from us? Why should I spend my money helping the damn employees?" he scoffs.

I hesitate, not wanting to anger him, but still needing to get my point across. "That idea may mean more money in the short-term, but I think throwing a bone to the workers is smarter. For one, we'll have higher caliber employees to choose from during hiring, because working here will be more desirable—cheaper housing is obviously a real benefit. And, it would mean better employee retention. People won't want to leave their jobs when they've got a solid and cheap place to live and a short commute."

My father looks pointedly over my shoulder and I turn my head, following his gaze. An entire spread of food sits on the white-marble kitchen island. I stand and walk over, noticing it's from Pastrami Queen, my favorite deli in New York City.

"I was wondering when you'd realize I put food out for you. I'm not a total fuck, ya know," he grunts.

I bristle, because that's exactly what he's become.

Letting my eyes take in what's before me, there are over-stuffed turkey and roast beef sandwiches, a mountain of fries, and three variations of their famous meat-stuffed knishes. Shit, he remembered the fried onion. A bunch of Diet Cokes sit in a bucket of ice. Even though I already ate, the growling in my stomach starts up again.

Grabbing a glass plate full of food and a cold can of soda, I settle back to the table. Before I take a bite, I notice how quiet it is. I haven't heard this kind of silence in years.

"Vincent," he sits up. "I know you're itching to get out of the city to run the business. But never forget where everything comes from." Carefully folding his hands together, he rests them on the table. "The money. The ability to start up. You wanna take the family into billions territory? Trust me—no one is complaining. But when we call on you to come back, you better run home. You're still my—"

I lift my right hand in the air, stopping him. "I was gonna wait to discuss this with you, but I guess now you've brought it up, then here we go. Once I'm out west, I'll take a decent cut and make sure to clean all the family money. I'll manage the Milestone to the best of my ability to make you rich. But the answer is a straight *no* about coming back to New York and sitting at the table."

He stares at me in disbelief. "The fuck you talking about? You don't go against my rule! I don't give a shit how angry you are about the BB working with us. You don't get to just wa—"

"I'm not sitting as your right hand," I tell him straight. "The family's changed since I went into lockup. And what's going on now isn't okay with me."

Turning my head toward the window, I notice a new large fountain installed; two huge pink and white marble angels embrace while water spills from their lips. Grimacing from the utter excess, I shake my head.

He slams his hand down on the table to get my attention, but I barely flinch. "You owe me your life, son. In more ways than you can fuckin' count. I groomed you for this role." He bares his teeth. "You don't get to just *choose*. You are the prince of this operation. Everyone knows who you are, especially after prison. Your days of hiding in school, not being marked—that's what's over," he huffs, pointing his finger at me. "You're home. And you belong. To. Me," he punctuates every word like a final decree.

"You can't control me," I steadily reply, maintaining a clear thought process. "I'm in the middle of building one of the largest casino complexes on the West Coast. No one else in the family has the aptitude for it. You want the money I'll bring in? You want a spot for your dirty cash? I'm your best option. Hell, I'm your *only* option," I reply in all honesty. "But the only way I'm doing this is if I take a step back and become a business partner with no other family ties. Otherwise—end my life. But good luck running the Milestone without me."

He balls his hand into fists. "You think you're the boss of me, making fuckin' choices? You think you can tell me what to do?" His face turns redder by the second. "I groomed you for this, Vincent. I. Made. You."

"You're working with untrustworthy lunatics—they're dirty. I told you that day in prison—I'll never work alongside the Boss Brotherhood," I growl.

He starts to laugh maniacally. "You'll regret this decision." His voice turns so low, I have to strain my ears to hear. "No one, and I mean no one, says no to Antonio Borignone."

The words "or else" are unspoken but dangle in the air like sharpened knives.

My chair grates against the floor as I stand. Walking over to the sink, I drop my plate inside before turning to walk away.

"Vincent," he calls out. I stop in my tracks. "You will not escape your destiny. I choose who comes and who goes. Who will live and who will die. Me." His jaw is clenched.

I shake my head at him. "I'd rather get taken in a body bag than live this life anymore. What you stand for won't be my way. I'm back, but I'm not the man I used to be. I won't eat your shit just because you plated it." I pause to gauge his reaction. His darkened eyes are trained on me. "I will continue to sit as the president of the Milestone as a business partner to you—only. No more family connection. I'm out."

His face breaks into a liquid slow smile full of threat. I choose to ignore it, turning away and leaving the kitchen to walk up another two flights to my old bedroom. Truth? I'm not afraid. I know my father loves money above all things. If for no other reason than to keep the cash coming in, he'll keep me alive. He's angry now, but as he gets richer, he'll calm down.

The amount of energy coursing through me is off the charts; I need to run. I open my bedroom door, pausing in the doorway. Peeking my head inside like an intruder, I note everything's the same. Still, it feels like another man's space. And metaphorically, it is.

My ornately carved wooden four-poster bed sits in the center of the room, covered in tightly tucked-in navy sheets. The red and blue Persian rug that Enzo bought for my sixteenth birthday covers the floor. A large antique bureau sits on the right corner by the window. On the opposite corner is a full computer system, just like he said.

I hesitantly step into the room and open my drawers to find fresh clothes. Pulling out a pair of black jersey shorts and a T-shirt, I press my nose to the small pile in my hands, shutting my eyes to take a deep inhale. The smell of fresh clothes? Heaven. Quickly changing, I run down to the windowless basement gym and alternate between running and lifting weights until I'm drained.

Dragging myself back upstairs, I tear off my sweat-drenched clothes and drop them in a pile on the bathroom floor before realizing the housekeeper must have come up while I was working out; four fresh towels sit beside the marble sink. I make a mental note to thank whoever's doing the cleaning.

Eagerly, I turn on the shower, fixing the dial so the water is hot. Before stepping in, I take a look in the mirror. It's been a while since I've really seen myself.

My six-foot-two frame is wider now—two hours a day of working out has its benefits. I'm solid muscle, more so than ever before; my six-pack has turned into an eight. My right arm is inked with the Borignone mafia insignia, Eve's name etched within the tribal design. I'll turn this tatt into something else. A sleeve, maybe. I glance down at my hip, touching the five-inch scar raised above my skin from a shiv. My mind roams back to the day in the yard when I was first approached by those Neo-Nazi fucks—the Boss Brotherhood.

I walk outside with my men behind me, the weather hot and stale. Like the chow hall, the entire yard is separated by race. Crow, president of the BB, saunters over to us; two of his boys with their heads shaved to the skin stand behind him like soldiers, ready to do his bidding. As the controllers of the tattoo shops and poker tables—as well as enforcing segregation— they're often referred to as the old white guard.

I make a mental note as to how different the family is from the other factions here. We live presentably and cloak ourselves in legitimacy. The

BB, though? They've got violent crime tatted all over them. In fact, the more obvious, the better off they think they are. Their style is extreme and carica-ture-like, so much so it's easy to dismiss them as absurd. But if I ignored them, I'd be making a mistake. Within these walls, the BB is a highly powerful group.

Crow lifts his hand in greeting. "Yo. Borignone. Let's go for a walk, eh?" He strokes his chin. I'd put him in his mid-thirties, although he could be younger. A hard life can age a man. A bold black swastika takes residence in the center of his pale throat next to the number 666. He sickens me.

I turn around, letting the guys know I'm going before giving Crow a small nod in agreement. We step away, walking toward the north side of the fence, facing C-Block.

"I think we could do some good shit together, Borignone," he starts, puffing out his chest.

I inwardly laugh. Over my dead body would I ever align with these pieces of shit.

He pivots to face me, standing ramrod straight. "How I see it is simple. Here on the inside, you and I are small in numbers, but strong. We can align. On the outside, you guys run guns up the West Coast. The BB would like to help you with that. Inside and out, we can benefit each other."

I keep my face passive and thoughtful as if I'm considering his proposal. Even though the answer is fuck-no, there's no use in creating enemies. "The family doesn't do work with outsiders. We've got our own routes and our own men. But I'll mention it to Antonio for you," I reply politically.

He squints his eyes, angered by my noncommittal response. "Well, I hear you can do more, eh? Or are you not as important as they're sayin'?" He moves to his tiptoes, obviously trying to get a rise out of me. I stand strong and silent, unmoving.

He gets within a few inches of my face. "You're the next king of the Borignone mafia. I may be living in prison, but I'm not under a fuckin' rock." His teeth are clenched as he speaks.

Silence, like heavy tar, sits between us before he lets out a slow and heavy chuckle. "Oh, I see. Daddy doesn't let you make any decisions, huh?" He points a skinny finger directly to my chest. "You're weak. Sent here to become a man, is that right?" He stares me up and down, laughing.

There are some truths in prison. The first one is the vulnerable get stomped. I've got to show this fucker and everyone who's watching I'm not to be messed with. I already know it's critical to fight as viciously as I can the first time I get into a confrontation. The best thing for me to do is act like I'm nothing but a sheep. Let him come at me and then, I'll show him what I can do.

He clenches his right fist. He must be holding a weapon. "You're a pansy, Borignone? Ready to take it up the ass, maybe? If that's what you like, I got boys I can arrange who'd love that GQ mug of yours. Maybe I'll even take a turn." He puts his hands down the front of his pants, grabbing his dick.

I take quick stock of his build; he's close to six feet and looks decently fit. I'm a few inches bigger, though. I purposely cower, trying to look scared. Meanwhile, I scan my surroundings to see if his crew is going to join him. I can feel a charge in the air. People seem to notice our tension and alerts have gone up among the prisoners. It's only a matter of time before the guards realize something's up. I don't have long to make this happen.

The animal inside me starts to pound as I keep my body steady, the beast within me ready to break free. I must maintain outward calm so he doesn't see my readiness.

I frown in mock fear. "Look, man," I start, darting my eyes around as if I'm scared. "I'm not gonna fight you. Let's just chill." I adjust my footing, waiting for him to jump.

He comes at me quickly, jamming a sharp object into my lower abdominals. It slices straight through my clothes and into my skin. He thinks he can hurt me? He has no idea who he's dealing with. I'm Vincent fucking Borignone! I see nothing but the blood I'm ready to spill.

Like a man possessed, I go after him, punching him so hard in the face I can hear a CRACK—shattering of bones. I grab his skinny throat with my opposite hand, squeezing until his lips turn blue. This time, I'm the one laughing as I smash the side of his head over and over again.

A swarm of guards surrounds us, but I easily pull back. My work is done. He coughs hard before moaning in agony, water and blood dripping from his nose and eyes. His face is obviously broken and dislocated, the *angle of his jaw harshly shifted from a few minutes ago. I'm smiling wide with adrenaline, staring at my blue shirt now stained black with blood.*

I spit on the ground, relieved to have solidified my place in this hellhole. I've made it clear I'm not afraid of anyone or anything. As the guards cuff me, I glare at every man ballsy enough to stare, telling them with my eyes: I will kill whoever stands in my way. There's only one alpha here—me.

The guards walk me to the infirmary and shackle me to the bed like the prisoner I am. After the doctor stitches my wound to stop the bleeding, I get sent underground to a blackened cell aptly named The Hole.

I sit in a concrete corner, shaking and sweating. Fever. How did my life land me here? My mind begins to struggle with the brutality of my hands. My father, blue eyes flashing as he locks me in the closet as punishment for disobedience. Faces of the men I've killed in the name of honor and allegiance. Piles of books in the school library. Professors lecturing to notetaking students. The man I always wanted to be, but couldn't reach...I'm so far away from him. Freedom, in the true sense of the word, will never belong to me—at least not so long as I represent the Borignone mafia. I'm staring at nothing but darkness, farther from redemption than I ever was.

On my knees, I pitch forward. Eve, oh God, she makes me whole. With her, I rise. I thought coming to prison was the right thing to do. The honorable thing. What a delusion I lived under. There's nothing here but death and degradation. I whisper prayers into the cell, begging for redemption as I roll in and out of consciousness.

* * *

I hear the shower running and I'm snapped back to the present. Moving inside the spray and shutting the glass door behind me, I groan in pleasure from the heat and hard water pressure. Damn, but this feels like heaven. The water rains down, coating me.

Shutting my eyes, I find peace with the image of Eve. I haven't said her name out loud since entering the Pen. My only fear in lockup was that my weakness of loving her would implicate her.

I drop my head, envisioning her in the shower. *She's on her knees...my cock feels so heavy in her mouth. I bring her up to standing and stare at her gorgeous wet body. I slide my hand down to her center, curling my fingers up the way she likes until she's writhing in my arms.* "I love you, Vincent. Don't stop. Don't stop..." *she's begging me. Needing me.*

"Oh, Fuck!" I groan. "Eve," I yell, her name echoing against the shower walls as I come undone.

2

EVE

6 Months Later

"Hey, Lauren," I knock on the corner of her desk as I walk through the office, black Louboutins clicking against the marble floor. The law office of Crier, Schlesinger, and Hirsch is located in Century City, the business district in Los Angeles. I work for Jonathan Foyer in the real estate department, assisting him in transactional work. He's the biggest and most well-renowned real estate attorney on the West Coast. Landing this job straight out of law school two years ago was a dream come true. Not only is the experience of learning from him completely invaluable, but the caliber of work is high.

After pulling out my cell phone and dropping it on my desk, I place my quilted red Chanel bag in the bottom drawer and immediately log onto my computer to check the week's work calendar. I pause, confused at what looks like major changes to the schedule. This better be a mistake.

Lauren struts into my office in a skirt-suit, her blonde hair pulled back in a low ponytail. She places a hot cup of coffee and a protein bar on my desk. I look up at her pointedly, my face tight.

"I've got three closings this week and need conference room A for the large screen. I requested it, but now it's blocked?"

Before she can answer, my phone rings. It's an unknown number —again. Someone has been calling me over the last few months, not leaving any messages. Refusing to answer any call from an unknown, I tap IGNORE.

Staring at Lauren, I let her know with my eyes that my question still stands.

She dismisses my forceful tone, understanding I'm in work-mode. Clients want an attorney who's a shark, and the other lawyers here would eat me alive if I didn't have skin as thick. The moment I walk into this office and sit in this chair, I have to put on my emotional armor.

Leaning onto my desk, a mischievous smile spreads across her Botox-filled face. Even though Lauren is only thirty-two, she's had so many fillers done I'd categorize her as ageless. Still, it's undeniable that she's a classic beauty.

Lowering her head closer to mine, I'm accosted by her Creed Spring Flower perfume. "Jonathan is on lockdown," she says conspiratorially. "Apparently, there's a new development and he's dying to get his hands on it. He's using conference room A for the rest of the week, and he's got the DBC in there with him right now. The developer is coming in at three o'clock this Friday."

"How long have they been strategizing? Those douchebags are always trying to cut me out of the big deals," I exclaim.

We call the three other associates in the transactional real estate department the DBC, for Douchebag Boys Club. I'd feel bad for the name, but the truth is they deserve it and worse.

Crier employs over twenty-five attorneys. There are five partners, and each has three to six lawyers working under them as associates. Four associates work under Jonathan, including me. Instead of working together, the dynamic is one in which everyone is always trying to get one up on the other. As if the workload wasn't stressful enough on its own, I have three cutthroat men who would step on my head with their suede Ferragamo loafers if it would enable them to rise in the ranks. We all started at the same time, but they like to see themselves as higher up and more important than me. Lauren, our legal secretary, is the only one I can trust.

I strum my freshly manicured nails on my desk, a nervous habit I acquired in law school. I can't remember if I've heard of any new developments big enough to warrant this level of Jonathan's anxiety. It's probably located outside of California. All of the attorneys on our team have passed New York and California bar exams at a minimum to enable us to close deals around the country; this project could technically be anywhere.

"What if he doesn't choose me to help him?" I ask anxiously, biting my bottom lip. On average this past year, I've billed mostly sixty-hour weeks, essentially bringing in millions of dollars for the firm in hours alone. I know Jonathan is happy with my output, but my goal is to make partner within the next five years. If a huge client comes in, I *must* be the lead associate working on it.

Lauren snorts, waving a hand in front of her face. "Those assholes can't get rid of you. They don't have your capacity in brains or work ethic. Jonathan has to choose you to work on this deal if he knows what's good for business." She winks, and I want to get up and hug her. Instead, I take a big bite of my chocolate-brownie protein bar.

She walks to the door and pauses. "Oh, and don't forget, hair and makeup are coming here for you at eight Friday night for the Kids Learning Club gala," she smiles. "I have your gown and a pair of Louboutin heels hanging in your closet." She points to the small door on the right side of the room where I keep spare clothes.

"Okay, good." I can continue working while the glam squad does its thing.

For the last four years, I spend my Monday and Wednesday nights working at the Kids Learning Club, helping teens prepare for college entrance exams like the SAT. I remember how it felt to study all night long on my own when I knew that rich kids were all being tutored for the same test; it gave them a leg up and frankly, it wasn't fair. By doing this, I feel like I'm leveling the playing field. Not least, I want the kids to know that changing their circumstances is possible. I tell each of them about my difficult upbringing so they understand that if I could do it, they can too. Mobility is possible.

Every spring, the Club holds a large fundraiser. While I'd rather spend a free night sitting at my kitchen table eating kabobs from the Persian restaurant down the block and reading a new romance on my Kindle, I would do anything to support these kids. If that means wearing a gown and schmoozing, so be it.

"Is Marshall picking you up from work beforehand?" Lauren asks excitedly, practically bouncing up and down on her toes. I roll my eyes. Marshall is a doctor, clean-cut and preppy—the type of man most women would be happy to introduce to their family. In my opinion, the best part about him is he's busy and so am I. He expects little from me, and I appreciate that enormously. I'm all work, all the time. The last thing I want, or need, is a clingy boyfriend. I just can't handle the pressure of a relationship or the vulnerability that comes with it. Not least, I don't think I have the capacity for love in that way. At least, not anymore.

"No, he'll meet me there," I reply.

"Too bad, I was hoping to see him." She looks at me pointedly. "You do realize that whenever I mention Marshall, you cringe?" She opens her mouth to say more, but thankfully, my office phone rings.

"Hello?" My voice is sharp as if I was in the middle of an important meeting and whoever called just disrupted me.

Lauren exits the room as Jonathan's voice comes over the line.

"Conference room A. Now."

I stand up, straightening my navy suit. It's perfectly tailored to my frame and the right blend between stylish, classic, and covered. It may not be exciting, but it works.

Grabbing my long yellow legal pad and a blue ballpoint pen, I walk across the carpeted hallway and into the conference room. The DBC are clustered closely around the large rectangular table, designer ties loose even though it's still morning. Files surround them.

I hesitate. How long have they been working without me? The door *clicks* shut and Jonathan looks up from his mountain of paperwork.

"Huge deal we're trying to land. Potential for years of billing; and that's without any lawsuits that will come up along the way. They want to open up their doors within the year, but they haven't actually closed tenants yet. We're looking at four hotels that need hospitality groups—huge closings. Huge." His smile is wide and unstoppable. The man is in his element right now.

"Read," he hands me a stack of files, with what looks like two-hundred-plus pages of documents. "Write up a summary of your findings—your most concise work. Fewer than thirty pages."

I can't escape the collective smirk of the DBC. They think they'll be talking and strategizing with Jonathan while I'm stuck reading in my office. But what they don't understand is I'm going to learn every single detail. And when Jonathan has a question, he'll always defer to me. I'll make myself invaluable to the project.

"No problem, Jonathan. When do you need this by?"

"Tonight," his voice is clipped. "Oh, and Eve? Bring coffees for all of us. Now."

I bristle as the DBC laugh under their breaths. I clench my fists in order to keep my calm. I won't jeopardize my career over being treated like a secretary from time to time. I'm tougher than that. And in the end, my persistence is what will bring me to the top. I just have to deal with this for a few more years and then I'll finally be treated with the respect I deserve. My past experience is actually helpful to me, because no matter how bad things get in this office, it's sunshine compared to the life I used to live.

I walk out of the room and drop the stack of files at my desk before walking to the small kitchen in the back of the office. I consider spitting into the carafe but decide against it. Returning to the conference room, I attempt invisibility. Brandon raises his eyebrows before his eyes dart to my ass; the asshole loves to watch me performing these menial tasks. I leave the coffee with a stack of fresh cups at the console and exit the room. I've got work to do.

I open up a Word document on my computer and stare at the stack of files for a moment; another person may be daunted, but working hard is part of my DNA. I blow the air from my lungs, readying myself to learn the entire history of this deal.

I kick my shoes off my feet beneath the desk, getting comfortable. The first stack I pick up is a contract between the Masuki Tribal Council and the Milestone, LLC. My eyes freeze on the cover page as my stomach does a slow churn. My fingers tremble as I open the file and begin to skim. The purpose of this contract is to build a large-scale casino and hotel complex.

I do a quick scan of the other documents, noticing his name isn't here; everything has been signed via Power of Attorney. Is this Vincent? I blink, clenching my fists. It can't possibly be him. He's been in prison. But why would someone have an agent do business on their behalf, if not because they're not in a position to handle things themselves? Normally, one uses a Power of Attorney if he is unable to handle his own affairs as a result of illness or old age. I guess, technically, Vincent may have chosen this avenue due to his absence. The agent would have been able to do anything Vincent requested. Like, for example, build a huge hotel and casino. Sign documents. Pull out money from banks. Request loans. If Vincent trusted this person, a lawyer from what I can tell, that man could have been Vincent's hands and feet on the ground while Vincent masterminded everything from behind bars.

I drop my head into my hands and swallow hard. "This is work," I tell myself out loud. "I'm putting my conspiracy theory behind me and getting it done."

By evening, the summary is complete. I immediately email Jonathan and within seconds, he replies with a confirmation. I shake out my shoulders, knowing I've got another few hours of work to complete for other clients.

Checking my phone, it's already nine o'clock. I'll just bring the rest back home with me so I can at least be comfortable.

I get into my black Mini Cooper and throw my bag and files into the seat next to me. With the blinding Los Angeles traffic, my mind roves to the man I've kept locked out of my consciousness; no amount of mental toughness will save me now.

I should just call Angelo and find out if Vincent is behind this. But what if he says, "Yes, it's him." My mouth dries.

The reality is—whether or not Vincent is part of this deal—it's actually none of my concern. He's an ex-boyfriend, and whatever happened in the past is over. I refuse to ever let myself go back into that black hole.

When I first got out to California, my life was in shambles. I was emotionally broken, physically weak, and all alone. I questioned myself a million times. Did he lie in order to make sure I left the East Coast or was the joke on me? Angelo's insistence that Vincent was never faithful made the waters harder to muddle through, and I suffered in that space between. Questioning. Constantly wondering.

The silver boot charm I found in my bag the day I left New York continued to burn a hole in my psyche. Night after night was sleepless and filled with a profound sense of helplessness—did he give me this charm, or did it simply fall off the keychain? If he gave it to me, what was he trying to say? Am I leaving him to rot in prison when I should be helping him? Guilt was one of the primary things I felt, as if I abandoned the love of my life.

My mind plays the word "no" on repeat. He cheated and lied; that's what Angelo swore. But my heart refused, and still refuses, to fully believe it.

Traffic lights switch from red to green and I pull over to the side of the road, not trusting myself behind the wheel right now. I shift my car into park and lean my head on the steering wheel before letting my thoughts wander back to that night, a month after arriving in California. I was nothing but a nineteen-year-old kid—heartbroken.

* * *

The beach is so dark. There are no stars in the sky, only the black expanse above. I focus on the curling ocean waves moving at a steady rhythm. Last week, Janelle told me our mother died of a drug overdose. She was dead for a long time in the apartment, but it took five days for someone to realize she was missing and go check on her. God, so much unfinished business between us. Should I have tried harder to help her? Did my leaving without a trace make her worse? For the second time in my life, I'm left to wonder if dying isn't the better option.

I dig my toes into the sand, the cold grains nestling between my toes. How am I going to live without Vincent? I gave him all of myself. And when he left to prison, he took the fabric of my insides with him. I'm nothing now but an empty casing. I can almost understand my mother's twisted solitude.

I strip naked as the salty wind rushes my limbs.

I don't know how to swim. Still, I want to go inside. If I drown? Relief hits me with the thought.

"Vincent," I cry, stepping into the cold, shallow water.

Trembling, I move deeper into the dark. "Vincent? Can you hear me?" I call out into the night, wondering if maybe he can feel me calling. I shiver.

With tears burning down my face, I continue my slow steps until the ocean pools around my thighs. Waves roll up to my breasts and back down again, leaving goosebumps in their wake. My nipples become painfully hard. It's so cold. Still, I welcome it. Should I go in farther? Yes. I continue to step forward.

In the distance, I hear the unmistakable song "Hot Line Bling"—my ringtone for Janelle. I want to ignore the call and keep walking, but the song persists, taunting me. "What if she needs me?"

Turning around to face the beach, I wrap my body with my arms and wade back through to the shore. The sand sticks to my legs, coating my feet and calves. I bend down to pick up the phone from the top of my clothes pile. The ringing is done, but there's a new text. It's Janelle, telling me to open my email. My body continues to tremble, wet and wind-chilled, but I click the envelope on the bottom of my phone screen. Reluctantly, I read.

Eve,
I can't sleep. I know you've been suffering and it kills me that you're all alone out there. Since Mom died, you've gotten worse. Angelo keeps calling,

too. I hoped that maybe when you left to California, you'd feel as though you were reborn or some shit. But I guess your demons have followed you. Mom hated you because you were better than her. She was jealous. We always ignored her abuse, but that's on me. I thought talking about it would make it all worse. I knew how badly she hurt you and the truth is, I should have done more to protect you. I know she's still sitting on your conscience, but I want you to kick her ass out! She's dead now, and I want all of her taunting to die, too. I know you're probably thinking you wish you did something else. Well, Eve, there's nothing you could have done. She was damaged goods, and honestly, I'm glad she's dead.

And Vincent, that motherfucker. You've been out in California a month now and still mentioning his dumb ass and questioning the truth. It's time to let him go. Tell yourself this: Regardless of what happened or didn't happen, the results are the same. Vincent is locked up and you're free. If he really cheated on you and all that, then fuck him—go live to spite him. And if he lied just so you'd move out to Cali, then live life FOR him. You see? No matter what the reasoning, the bottom line is LIVE LIFE.

Now, I want you to read through this list of dares and swear to me you'll complete them. Maybe it'll give you the push you need to finally step out of your depression.

Monday: Spend twenty minutes today making friends with the girl who lives next door to you

Tuesday: Get a guy in one of your classes to join you for a day at the beach

Wednesday: Ask two girls on your floor for dinner

Thursday: Pick up your books and study in the library—not in one of the closed rooms, but on the main floor where everyone talks; no headphones

Friday: See a movie with the girl who lives across the hall

Saturday: Go to a frat house with a new friend and drink a beer

By the way—the weather sucks in New York.

Love ya!

I sob hysterically as I put my clothes back on over my damp skin and head home in a daze. Another girl may be afraid of walking unaccompanied in darkness, but I've been through worse. And I'm not afraid of death.

The next morning, I wake determined to follow Janelle's orders. I'm not *sure if I could ever fall out of love with Vincent, but maybe I can find someone or something to help lessen the pain.*

That night, I kiss a stranger at a party; it feels awkward. It's my attempt at assuming the ritual of a typical college girl. The girls in my dorm do this all the time, and they seem to be carefree and without troubles, lighthearted and living a life where nothing is taken too seriously. A hookup gone wrong is hilarious. Sex with someone's boyfriend is due to drunkenness. Life is simple.

The clock ticks and time passes. Who am I?

It's Friday night. I walk into a party on campus with my friends when I see a man. He's tall and dark. Built. "Who's that?" I ask Molly, my neighbor in the dorms.

"That's James Dogman. He's the lacrosse captain." She bobs her head up and down. "Crazy hot, right?"

I don't respond.

Physically, he resembles Vincent more than anyone else I'd ever seen. My traitorous body hums. I feel disloyal. Still, I'm dying to feel an emotion other than emptiness.

He catches my stare and smiles, a deep dimple forming in his left cheek. He pushes through the crowd, seemingly to get to me. This man is bigger than everyone else by at least five inches. He takes my hand, knowingly, and walks us to the staircase. It's quieter here. He makes a joke and I laugh. He asks about my major. I tell him pre-law. He asks for my number and I give it. He tells me to take his too, and I say, "Okay."

"You're fuckin' gorgeous." His voice isn't deep like Vincent's.

He moves his hand to touch my hair and I quickly tie it back in a low ponytail. He looks at me funny, but I smile like it's nothing.

The lights are off. I'm burying myself into his wide muscled chest. His smell, a fancy and sharp cologne, is all wrong. I look into his dark brown eyes, searching for a connection. But all I find is a stare as empty as my heart.

I leave before he wakes, shaking with stress as I dress and telling myself that it will be better next time.

The following week, he asks me to his game. I watch him from the stands with friends, doing my best to have fun. We draw hearts on our faces in the school's colors, posing for photos and taking selfies. But it's all a ruse. Turns out, I'm good at faking it. Weeks pass, and he notices nothing.

A month goes by. Everyone tells me I'm so lucky. I internally shrink.

Another night. Movies and chill. James is above me, but my mind starts playing tricks. It's James, and then it's Carlos. Naked and sweating, pushing against me. Hurting me. Tattooed teardrops down his wild eyes. I'm too afraid to scream.

With a burst of energy, I push all two-hundred-some pounds of man off me. Jumping out of his bed, I trip over my own feet as I dress in panic. Underwear. Jeans. Bra. Tank top. My heart—it may explode. I hear static. Running down the steps of his off-campus house, I sprint to my dorm, sweat pouring down my face. I go straight into the shower, turning the dial to scalding. I drop on the tiled floor, clothed and crying.

I finally get back to my room and dial Janelle. I'm shivering.

"Eve, please speak with a therapist. You still have so much unresolved shit, and it's all catching up."

I hang up.

I need to move on again and find a new set of friends. Still, I want to try to live. I want to be happy. James keeps calling, but I avoid him.

Vincent invades my dreams. I hate that I can't let him go. All I want is to forget him! But he plagues me.

Vincent's hands...Vincent's eyes...Vincent's voice.

"You're young," Janelle reminds me the following day over the phone. "You'll find a new man again; I swear it."

"Angelo sent me care packages of expensive clothes and makeup. He even sent me a fancy coffee maker. Do you think he's doing all of this because he feels guilty about lying?" I lift up a gorgeous pair of J Brand jeans as I hold the phone between my ear and shoulder. "Maybe all this stuff is his form of apology."

"No, Eve," she insists angrily. "It's because he wants you comfortable. Why is that so hard to imagine? Angelo loves you. That's why he sends you stuff."

I need to believe her. But deep down, I don't. "You're right. I'm being crazy."

A few weeks later, I'm hanging out with my new friends, who are inter-

ested in philosophy and being "deep." They all grew up in cushy households but love to talk about the "struggle," as if they'd been there. We get high on Mexican marijuana while sitting on five-thousand-dollar couches and discussing the merits of higher tax rates for the rich. I stay quiet, leaning on a beautiful silk pillow. Missy told me earlier that it's Armani home. I'll need to look that up.

I take a sip of my fancy imported beer, reminding myself that I'm lucky. I have a life. I'm not lying in a ditch in the Blue Houses or floating in the Hudson River.

Life goes on in a rhythm of classes and parties. A year passes by. And another. And slowly, the ache for Vincent starts to numb. The want and the need—that never leaves. But the heaviness in my heart is lessening. It's almost as though my body went through an unconscious healing process where all emotion was crushed out of my body. I'm harder now, but at least I'm not crumbling.

* * *

A car honks its horn and I'm brought back to the moment. "I'm not a kid anymore. I'm a woman now," I exclaim into the empty car, slamming the steering wheel with the palm of my hand.

The me of seven years ago would be out of my mind with this new information. The old me would be wracked with tremors with her head in the toilet, vomiting from the stress. But the me of today is able to rise above the pain. Maybe it isn't Vincent behind this deal. And if it is? I wouldn't be the first person to work with an ex-boyfriend. I'll just figure it out, like I have everything else in my life. I will not allow this problem to become me. It's simply just an event in my life and I will deal with it as such.

I have a job that pays more money than I ever dreamed, a nice boyfriend, who may not give me toe-curling sex, but it's still good enough. I even have an apartment, which I bought all on my own. I shut my eyes, focusing on the feeling of relief and safety. When I'm centered, I pull back into traffic and resume the drive to my apartment.

Friday morning comes faster than I'd hoped. I go through my usual morning routine of a hot cup of coffee at six o'clock while skimming the news headlines on my phone. After my three-mile treadmill run, I take a hot shower followed by a quick blow-dry of my hair. My tan skirt-suit is impeccably tailored and I know I look both professional and stylish. After securing my hair in a tight and sleek bun, I apply Bobby Brown tinted moisturizer all over my face, NARS concealer under my eyes, and Two-Faced bronzer beneath the hollow of my cheekbones. Work at the firm is a battle, and my hair, makeup, and clothes are my shields.

The entire office is buzzing when I walk in, the possibility of landing the Milestone is obviously generating excitement. Lauren and I make eye contact as she jumps up from her desk.

Walking a step behind me, she starts without any preamble. "The meeting has been shifted to nine thirty."

My head is down, eyes glued to my phone as she hands me a cup of coffee. I put out my right hand to take it from her. "Did you get the file for Bearwoods Resort?"

Lauren has a friend at the firm, Scranton and Arps, who did work on another casino complex on Native American lands. I knew it would be a big help for me to review a development that is comparable to the Milestone.

"Yup. It's on your chair. Everything that's not confidential." I look up as she winks, letting me know with no uncertain terms that the entire file is there, confidentiality be damned. It's a dog-eat-dog world I work in, but as Jonathan always says: If you don't play, you can't stay.

I finally take a seat at my desk and Lauren hands me my protein bar before quickly leaving the room. I always need quiet before a big client comes in; silence helps me focus.

I take a sip of coffee before shutting my eyes. Leaning my elbows on my desk and massaging my temples with my fingertips, I repeat: It's just a client. I can handle it.

My door swings open. It's Lauren.

"Oh my God!" she exclaims. "I know I shouldn't be in here when you're doing your mind focus or whatever, but holy shit!" She leans against the door, fanning herself with two hands. I take a deep inhale through my nose. It's *him*. The blood in my veins turns cold as I swallow the bile rising in my throat.

"The man outside. Holy hell!" She practically skips to my desk in excitement. "You know those guys that are all dirty and rough? Like, he looks like he probably smokes a pack a day for breakfast, fucks you ten ways by lunch, and works hard labor under the sun?"

"Jesus, Lauren. You're out of your mind." I let out a shaky laugh.

"Oh, come on. You know what I mean. The guy out there for the Milestone. He's like, dark and brooding. Like he hasn't shaved in a week because he's too cool to care. His sleeves are rolled up and his forearms are all corded muscle and all these black tribal tattoos! And not like these hipsters. He looks like the real deal. I'm equal parts turned on and scared right now. I bet his dick is like, a foot long. So hot!"

"When's your romance novel coming out Lauren Love Joy?"

She puts a hand on her slim hip. "Oh, please. When you see him, you'll understand. Trust me on this, Eve. He's the kind of hot that any straight breathing woman can appreciate." She's absolutely giddy.

Before I can speak, my door reopens. It's Jonathan in a perfectly tailored navy suit with his lucky blue silk tie. "Hey sweetheart, it's show time," he exclaims.

Jonathan loves this part; wheeling, dealing, and finessing are his specialties. I remind myself to calm down. *It doesn't matter if Vincent is here. This is my life's work, and nothing he can do will take this away from me.*

Entering the conference room, I smile at Jonathan and the rest of the real estate team, who sit facing the door. I stand tall, channeling serious and sophisticated attorney. It's a role I can play. Before I round the table to take my seat next, Jonathan pipes up.

"Eve, before we begin, can you get all of us coffees please?" His voice is my command.

I turn on my heel and run into the kitchen, willing my heart to slow down as I pour the coffee into the carafe. Re-entering the room, I do my best not to trip. Even though I see the DBC chuckle to each other, because apparently me carrying their coffee never stops being funny, I keep my back straight and pretend I don't notice.

Jonathan already set my legal pad in front of my chair. I take my seat and immediately drop my head to review my notes.

A throat clears and my head pops up. My eyes practically bug out of my skull and a soundless gasp comes flying from my mouth. Gone is any resemblance to the man I knew. The lower half of his face is covered in dark scruff; if not for his sharp cheekbones and eyes, he'd be unrecognizable.

As his deep and soulful stare bores into mine, I know he hasn't changed much at all. All at once, I'm that innocent girl again. Small pieces of me that have been dormant for years vibrate in my chest. With just one look, Vincent moves me. He's coarser but still utterly gorgeous. There's a hardness about him now, which wasn't there before. Clearly, prison changed him. But I guess I've changed, too. *Can he see me?*

Jonathan clears his throat. "Vincent, this is Eve. She's an attorney on our team." Vincent leans forward and we each put out our hands to shake. The moment he takes my hand, a spark of an electrical charge surges through my body before simmering into a warm and slow buzz. A few seconds pass and my palm is still encased in his; he isn't letting me go.

Nervously, I wriggle my hand free. Sitting back in my seat, I feel like crying. Anger boils up on sadness's heels.

I can't believe he has the audacity to show up at my work. I harden like I've trained myself to do. A shadow crosses his face as he realizes I'm closing myself off from him. I want to stomp my feet and scream, "I'm not a naïve little girl living in the projects! I'm not the girl you knew."

Jonathan continues to introduce Vincent to the rest of the team. "Vincent is the man behind what will be the most incredible hotel and casino complex in the country. It's really an honor to meet you." Jonathan is in full kiss-ass mode.

Vincent lifts a hand politely in thanks before casually resting one foot on his opposite knee. Raw masculinity drips from his pores while his eyes are savagely trained on me. As if he's able to control me with only a heated look, my entire body floods back to life. I cross my legs tightly, telling the pulsing ache in my lower body to stop. But of course, the little traitor doesn't listen.

For years now, I just assumed I wasn't a sexual person. I chalked up my time with Vincent as adolescent excitement, figuring adult relationships don't have that kind of heat. Wild attraction is for kids, not adults with mortgages.

And now, with one look at Vincent, my blood stirs straight into my core, abruptly waking up my sexuality without consent.

I'm snapped out of my trance as Jonathan speaks. "Eve. Offer him a drink." I stand.

Vincent squints as if confused, turning his dark gaze to Jonathan. "Didn't you just tell me she's one of the attorneys here?"

Jonathan smirks. "Yes, but she helps us out too from time to time. You know how it is." He laughs jokingly. His implication that I do more than work as an attorney is obvious, and I cringe.

Vincent's face turns to ice, his eyes darkening. *Oh shit.*

"No, I'm not sure what you mean. You want to elaborate?" His glacial eyes focus on Jonathan and it's as if the whole room stopped breathing.

Most of the time when Jonathan makes these comments, the businessmen laugh. It becomes a boy's club, and I'm the woman on the outs. I'd never do anything sexual to get my way, but apparently, just the joke is enough to bond them. I have to work harder than everyone else to prove I'm more than what they see. It's a vicious cycle, but what choice do I have? I try to show the clients I'm highly qualified via my strong work ethic, but it's difficult to get respect when Jonathan and the DBC make underhanded and subversive comments meant to disparage. I'm certain, though, I'll prove myself to all of them—eventually. I *have* to.

When Vincent decides Jonathan looks scared enough, he rises from his seat. Jonathan is straight-up terrified; I see the sweat beading on his forehead. He isn't sure if Vincent is about to kick him in the face or leave the office. Knowing Jonathan, he'd rather take a beating than lose this deal. Instead, Vincent moves swiftly to the console, pouring two coffees. One is black, but he adds milk and a spoon of sugar in the second. It's exactly the way I used to drink my coffee— and still do. He places the cup in front of me, making sure not to spill a drop.

"For you," he whispers, looking into my eyes. I feel lightheaded as he takes his seat.

Moving along like nothing is amiss, Jonathan continues with a smile, adjusting his tie self-consciously. "Let me introduce the rest of our team." He clears his throat.

Pointing to each person one by one, he states their respective title. When he gets to me, I raise my head, but can't manage to make any eye contact with Vincent; the stress is unbearable.

"So, you met Eve a few moments ago." I want to laugh out loud, but thankfully keep it in check. "She has her undergraduate degree from Stanford and JD from Stanford as well. She specializes in real estate transactions."

I see Vincent's face from the corner of my eye, lips twisted into a half smile.

"I heard about her work from a friend of mine, Colin Vorghese. He told me she's quickly becoming the best in the field. If I hire you, Eve must work on the Milestone with you."

I blink quickly. Did I hear him correctly? "Of course, she will." Jonathan's voice has an excited boom. I feel lightheaded. "Eve is fantastic. She'll be with you the entire way."

The eyes of the DBC pop in shock before a few chuckles fill the room.

I can see the indignation rise in Vincent's face as understanding dawns as to what these assholes may be thinking. "Yes," he states firmly. "What she was able to negotiate for Colin was outstanding. He and his wife are close friends of mine, and they both thought Eve's professionalism, work ethic, and intelligence is rare. I can use any other firm, but Colin insisted she and you, Jonathan, are the best team in the business." Vincent stares at Jonathan before glaring at the other attorneys, daring them to say otherwise.

"I'm glad Colin was happy. Keeping clients satisfied is what we do. So, Vincent." Jonathan claps his hands together. "Let's get to it."

Vincent sits up, explaining the Milestone, which he calls *the Mile* for short. He's in complete control. The room is hyper-focused as he maps out the intricacies of the Tribe and the detailed level of work needed.

I find myself completely engrossed in the details, taking copious notes and trying to stay calm and cool. Vincent begins to ask probing questions about how our team operates: timetables and friendships with state officials. Jonathan responds easily. He may be an asshole, but he knows his stuff.

By the end of the hour, my fingers are cramped from note taking and my lower back is damp. One thing is clear: if we get this deal, we'll be working non-stop for Vincent for a few years at a minimum; the workload is enormous.

Vincent stands to shake our hands as he readies himself to leave. Again, he takes mine for a second longer than necessary. His scent hits my nose like an aphrodisiac, woodsy and dark and something uniquely *him*. Everything about this man is like no one and nothing else. He finally lets go, turning to walk out the door with Jonathan at his heels. And just like that, he's gone.

A few minutes later, Jonathan returns to the room, loosening his tie and dropping into the chair at the head of the table. "So, you think he'll hire us?" he asks, his mouth set in a straight line, eyes filled with an emotion close to anxiety.

Jonathan is so successful precisely because he's always nervous he may not close the deal. That small piece of humility keeps him working harder than anyone else in the game.

Jeff clears his throat, crossing one skinny leg over the over. "Well, I think he'll come because we're the best. But I'm no longer sure we want his business."

Jonathan stares at him incredulously. "Explain."

"I heard to get his foot in the door out in Nevada, he used serious gang connections. You all may not be familiar with the Borignone mafia, but they're the most powerful gang on the East Coast." He moves his arms in front of his chest haughtily.

Now that Vincent requested me to work on the project, Jeff has the audacity to try to stop the entire firm from getting the work. *Selfish douchebag.* A nagging voice inside my head tells me to agree with him; working with Vincent would be the worst idea on earth. This could be my out. But the words won't leave my lips. I can't. I just can't do it.

Instead, I sit up taller. "Who mentioned anything about mafia connections?" I hate his snide remarks, and I refuse to let them stand, even if they're true.

"Well, things out there on the reservation aren't exactly kosher, Eve." His condescending tone is infuriating. "The Tribal Council was sitting on that land for years. Word on the street is the Borignone mafia had the rivers running red until the Tribe agreed to give Vincent a seat at their table.

"According to my research, Vincent is the son of the big Boss, Antonio Borignone. But because his mother was Native, he has a technical stake in the lands. He graduated from Columbia and proceeded to spend half a decade in prison for a laundry list of illegal dealings. And let the record show, his probation was done just last week." He lets his eyes roam the room, making sure we're all paying attention.

I swallow. It feels like I have a pit stuck in my throat.

"Sure, the man is obviously brilliant," he continues. "Managing to build out the entire Milestone while behind bars couldn't have been easy. But think about his reach," he exclaims, throwing his hands into the air theatrically. "A normal man, no matter how intelligent, could never pull that off. Vincent Borignone is a bona fide thug." He spits out his words confidently as if he's making a closing argument in front of the jury.

I click my tongue. "Interesting how this information never left your mouth until after he said he wanted to work with me," I question. "I've read the entire file from the beginning and know for a fact that every detail of the Milestone was done legally. Nothing shady—

at all. What he chooses to do on his time outside of this work is not our concern."

"I don't even want to know how many men were paid off or died so he could sit at the Tribe's table as a Council member." He turns to face Jonathan. "Are you sure you want to get involved in a business which could result in a gun to your head? The Borignone mafia is not a simple street gang. They're internally organized and smart. And they have no qualms in killing to get their way." He looks to the other associates, garnering their support. They shuffle nervously in their seats, obviously affected.

I'm outraged. "You shouldn't slander a potential client. It's totally unprofessional."

He laughs out loud. "You're calling me unprofessional? I can only imagine what Borignone is expecting to get from you in addition to legal work, huh?"

My jaw drops as a smile spreads across his face. If I could, I would jump over this table and knock out his teeth. This is a new low, even for Jeff.

"Enough," Jonathan says dismissively as if the conversation were nothing more than banter between two kids. "I don't care what he does on his own time. This man will make all of us rich if we get his work."

I'm shaking with fury. Jeff is only mad because I'll be center on this project and not him. But with enough time and hard work, my results will do the talking for me.

I wish I could report this to a higher-up, but the result would be a mark on my head. People will think I screamed "harassment" in order to grow in the firm. They'll spread rumors about me through the legal community, which is a small one. I'll never be able to get another job again. My rational mind tells me to just pick up and find another firm. But Crier is the best and my pay is unrivaled. In a few years, I can make partner and all of these issues will disappear. *They have to.*

We all leave the conference room and head to our respective

offices. I shut my door behind me before pulling down the blinds and bursting into tears.

And Vincent...how could he be here? My heart races.

My mind goes back to the night I found him sitting on the bed we shared, a bottle-blonde on her knees before him.

The fallout.

I was unable to shower or eat.

Daniela's onslaught of bullying—throwing salt over the burns Vincent created.

The entire school calling me "whore" to my face.

Imprisoning myself in my dorm when I wasn't in class.

My chest clenches with memories. All of my carefully crafted walls vibrate with Vincent's reappearance in my life. My stomach cramps.

I run to the bathroom and drop to my knees onto the green and pink tile floor, emptying the contents of my stomach.

3

VINCENT

I shift uncomfortably in the black Escalade, still reeling after seeing Eve for the first time in years, wondering how it's possible for a woman to be so beautiful.

I want to storm back into her office and throw her over my shoulder. Lock her in my hotel room and fuck her for hours on end. Make love to her deep and slow, how she loves. My dick hardens and I groan. With a curse, I tell myself I've got to keep it together, at least until I get back to my hotel room.

Every single piece of that woman calls to me, both in mind and body. Just the way she listened as I spoke, taking copious notes and biting on her plump bottom lip...I saw the way her eyes took me in; she is still attracted to me. But, there was something else in her gaze too, and it wouldn't take a genius to figure out it's the pain I caused all those years ago. Buried under a ton of tough-girl concrete is damage, and it'll take serious thought as to how I can fix it. Will she even let me?

Ideas bounce around my head, but I need to think on them—analyze the possibilities of where certain paths would take us and figure out which plan has the highest likelihood of bringing her back to me.

Slade is calling, but I hit IGNORE. I'm too shaken up after seeing Eve to speak with anyone.

He and I met at the gym shortly after I got out of prison. The gym's owner told me he had come home from Iraq a few months earlier and was working as an MMA instructor while he sorted out his life.

His demeanor was angry as hell. With dark circles under his eyes, a perpetual sneer on his face, and body completely ripped with heavy muscles, he had brutality written all over him. In other words, he looked like the perfect sparring partner.

My stress about Eve was compounding by the day, along with pressure from my father to keep myself in the family fold. Probation made me feel like a dog on a leash; I couldn't get to my girl and I was stuck under my father's shadow. Training to fight was the only stress release.

At about six feet and two hundred pounds of pure muscle and an obvious slew of anger management issues, Slade was a beast in the ring—exactly what I hoped he would be. After one crazy bout, I asked him how he got to be so good. Turns out he was on the boxing team in the Navy. Later that night, we grabbed dinner and surprisingly, he was a pretty decent guy. It didn't take long for hanging out to become a weekly occurrence. Soon after, we both opened up about the shit we faced, finding more similarities between ourselves than I would have predicted.

Eventually, I introduced him to Tom, who immediately trusted him. Slade's quiet, strong, and honorable in the way we were raised to understand honor.

Last month, I let Slade know I would need someone to run security at the Milestone and he jumped at the opportunity. For me, it was the perfect setup. He's a natural leader, smart, hardworking, and has all kinds of amazing connections because of his military background.

And for Slade, working with me out in Nevada was the opportunity of a lifetime. He had no family or close friends on the East Coast and hated working at the gym.

With the steady pace of the car, my mind turns back to the first time Slade gave me information on Eve.

* * *

Vincent: Yo. You around? Meet me at the gym.
Slade: Be there in 20

I shuffle to the white cement wall, placing my phone and a bottle of water on the short ledge.

Stepping to the heavy bag, I stretch for a moment to warm up. I'm planning on going harder tonight than usual, and don't want to get myself hurt by starting cold.

I finally begin, my fists moving faster and faster against the red bag. I want to keep focused, but it only takes a minute for the bag to turn into a set of bars. The men I killed in the name of the family. The time in lockup I did for the goddamn family. The girl I lost because of the fucking family. Anger crawls in my chest as I realize how much of my life I gave up in the name of loyalty.

I punch harder, heaving as sweat pours down my face as I add in various combinations. The physical intensity should shut my mind up, but it's not working.

Eve is now an adult. A woman with her own life. And what if she doesn't want me? I'm an ex-con. A reformed killer. I tore her heart out. She has no idea I did it to save her life. I've got to be a better man for her, but I can't when I'm still locked in New York. Fuck! I continue, punching harder and harder, welcoming the burn in my forearms.

Resting my bare hands on my knees, sweat drips from my forehead onto the mat below me. I lift my head. Slade's already here; he's watching me with lowered brows. Heavily tatted-up arms are crossed in front of his chest, a thoughtful expression on his face. Shaking his head from side to side, he gives me the cue to take a break.

Stepping closer, his dark eyes zero in on my knuckles. "Glad to see you stopped wrapping your hands with tape. Your grip will get much stronger this way." Pointing to my water bottle on the window ledge, he walks over and picks it up. "*Hydrate.*"

I grab the bottle from his hands, my big shoulders shifting beneath by soaked shirt.

"Ready to hear about your girl? I got good info from my boys out in Cali."

"Yeah, man. Yeah." I take another deep pull from the water bottle. The private investigator who works for the family is undeniably good, but I didn't want anyone finding out how desperate I've been to learn about Eve; getting her back on my father's radar is the last thing I would do. I did all the internet searching I could on my own but wanted to wait until I met someone I could trust before doing actual digging.

He leans against the cracked white wall as I pour more water down my throat.

"She's doing well. Still close to Angelo. Her phone records show calls at least once a month to him."

"Good. I was hoping Angelo would keep taking care of her," I murmur to myself.

"Your girl also managed to finish her undergraduate degree in two and a half years and went directly to law school. She's now working at one of the best law firms in the country doing real estate transactional work out in L.A."

I already knew this from my own searches but hearing it out of Slade's mouth has my chest filling with deep pride.

"She volunteers twice a week at the Kids Learning Club in Los Angeles as a tutor for underprivileged kids. Place is pretty run down, but she goes on Mondays and Wednesdays. As far as relationships are concerned, she's got herself a boyfriend. Been with him for a few months now. Last few years it's been a string of nice guys who come in and out of her life. This new one's a doctor at Sinai."

I face him, crunching the now empty bottle of water in my hands. "I'll head over to California this week."

His eyes flash, startled. "Fuck no," he exclaims. "You aren't risking your probation."

My heart beats erratically. "You don't understand what we went through. She and I. We were only kids. I-I fucked up. She was everything. And I—" I start sweating again.

He pats my shoulder with his hand. "I know, brother." His voice is calm as he presses his lips together. "You've explained the situation. But this is how I see it. Your girl's life was shit and she's finally gotten to a good place. Okay, so she's been with other guys. So fuckin' what?" He shrugs. "You can go get her again, but when you do, it's gotta be maturely. Not when you're out on parole, true?"

I know he's right. When I go back for her, it's gotta be at a time when shit is clear. I'm a man now, no longer an irrational kid.

"I'll keep watching her. Don't worry." He turns his face to the center of the gym. "Time to work."

We don't spar, but instead, put ourselves through treadmill sprints and weighted sled pushes. With each passing minute, the pain sets deeper in my chest until I swear to God I feel like I've got a gaping hole in my center. After forty minutes, he grabs a towel to head out.

"You gotta stop, man. It's enough."

"Nope," I reply easily, not nearly exhausted enough to give up. I step back onto the treadmill and turn up the speed, ready for more.

* * *

I get into my hotel room and unbutton my shirt, immediately calling Slade. He answers with a "Yo," and I begin without preamble.

"She's changed, man."

"It's been seven years. Don't tell me you thought you'd see the same college girl you knew."

I drop into a chair by the window, imagining her beautiful face.

"So now you've seen her. You still want to hire her? There are lots of other—"

"Yup."

"Honestly, I'm surprised she didn't throw her legal pad at your head when you walked inside," he chuckles.

"Need her schedule," I grunt. Lucky for me, Slade hacked into her work computer and Outlook account.

"Already got it. I'll shoot you an email now."

I hang up. Opening my laptop and clicking on the browser, I immediately find his email in my inbox. Turns out Eve has a black-tie event tonight with the Kids Learning Club at the Beverly Hilton.

I move to the edge of the white queen-sized bed with my laptop open. I know I shouldn't show up to an event Eve's at; I mean, that's stalker shit right there. Then again, it'll give me a chance to see the new woman she's become. I won't stay long. Just long enough to see what she's like in a social setting so I can plan the right way to get her back. There's only so much information photographs and schedules can give me.

I abruptly stand, feeling antsy. Pacing the room in long strides, I walk from one end to the next. I always think better when I'm moving.

The truth is that yeah, I want to see her. I want to grab her and fess up to all the dirty lies I told all those years ago. But I can't rehash all that shit. If I come to her all intense like I did in college, she'll run away. The last thing she wants—or needs—is a redo of a relationship that ended in heartache. No. If I do this, it has to be wisely. I'll come to her as a new man, through business, in a setting she's comfortable and confident in. Slowly, I'll slide myself back inside her heart. When the time is right, I'll tell her the truth about how I left things before prison. I won't just shove it down her throat or force her to believe me. The truth has to be revealed organically.

I used to be an aggressive, angry kid with no self-control. I want to show her how I've grown up. I crack my knuckles, finally feeling secure in this plan. I can't force her back to me. She needs to realize on her own that the love we shared was true.

Still, I want to see her tonight. No damn way I'm sitting alone in a hotel room when Eve and I are in the same city. I pick up the room phone, dialing the concierge.

"Hello, Mr. Borignone. How may I help you?"

"I need a tuxedo for this evening."

4

EVE

I'm still at my desk when a hair stylist and makeup artist strut into my office side by side, each rolling a small black suitcase behind her. It's after six, and the Kids Learning Club gala starts in a little over two hours. Luckily, I already have my gown, shoes, and bag all hanging in my office closet, courtesy of Lauren. Seriously, I need to thank that girl. If not for her, I'm not sure how I'd manage a life outside the office. The gift cards over Christmas just aren't enough.

I raise my head, acknowledging their entry.

While still at risk for breaking down in tears, I continue to use my coping skills to keep my emotions afloat. Rule number one: Don't stop working, and keep your eyes glued to the page. Currently, I'm reviewing a contract for a lease assignment. It's boring as hell, but it's what I do.

"Eve, right?" the taller girl asks, bringing my focus back to her. She bites her cheek nervously. Wearing her hair long and wavy with ends dipped in pink, she stares at me with wide eyes, as though I may bite her head off.

The second girl wears a micro-mini skirt, short black combat boots, and a torn T-shirt. "I'm makeup," she says, blinking behind two pounds of black mascara and a heavy row of false lashes.

I exhale, trying to relax the hard edges of my face; it's difficult to morph from high-strung attorney to easygoing and friendly. "Yeah, I'm Eve. You guys can set up over here behind me in front of the window. I'll continue to work while you do your thing." I force my lips into a smile.

"Great!" they reply in unison, looking relieved by the change in my demeanor.

Crouching down on the floor behind me, I hear unzipping. The tall one moves beside me, placing a flat iron, curling iron, a large round brush, and a blow dryer at the edge of my desk.

The girls are likely around my age of twenty-six. But where they're seemingly young and fresh and full of dreams, I'm working like a dog for a goal I'm not even sure I want anymore.

I make a few hundred thousand dollars a year as an attorney, plus a bonus. I should feel fulfilled; after all, I worked like hell to get to this spot. But deep down, I'm unhappy. They treat me like shit here. And while I'm learning a lot, I'm not remotely interested in what I'm absorbing.

I wanted to make it to this level in my career precisely so I could have stability and freedom—and I have it now. After going to college and graduate school with the upper-crust crowd, I yearned for this exact life of ease. Fancy dinners, beautiful clothes, and an apartment of my own. I thought I'd finally be happy but instead, there's only emptiness.

I stare at my computer screen, forcing myself to read while the girls prep my face for makeup and spritz my dry, but clean, hair with water.

"Girl, you are so lucky," she separates my thick locks into sections using a comb and clips, "to have this office! You must be so smart."

A cold hand spreads cream all over my face. "You're a girl boss!"

"We all work hard." I try to keep my face unaffected as she preps it for makeup. "My sister does hair in New York; so trust me, I know how hard you guys run. Don't tell her though, but New York doesn't hold a candle to L.A. beauty."

"Yasss," they exclaim, slapping each other five. "Where are you going tonight?"

"The Kids Learning Club gala."

"We just did another girl for the same event. But don't worry, you're hotter and you've got the better career."

We all laugh, but inside, my chest sinks. I want to tell them it's all just a façade. I'm not as happy as I seem. Instead, I just smile.

"How do you want to do your hair? I think beach waves would suit you best. Your bone structure is perfect for that look."

"Oh, and a smoky eye!"

"No," I reply firmly. "I want to go for straight and sleek. I want both hair

and makeup to be elegant, clean, and polished. Not too much bronzer. No sparkle." They both nod quietly in understanding.

The days of wild and sexy hair and makeup are firmly behind me. My New-York self is a time of life I'd prefer never existed. But somehow, the more I try to ignore the old me, the more she haunts me.

5

VINCENT

Eve walks into the ballroom and my heart constricts. In a long black gown, she is a sight to behold. She's straightened that wild hair I love. I smile with the memory of how hard she always tried to tame it down. But I always loved her exactly as she was, without all the bullshit other girls do.

My tux fits like a glove—an overly restrictive and scratchy one. I always hated dressing like this, and it's even more hellish now. I've got no patience for this shit. I lean against the darkly polished wooden bar, ordering a vodka rocks from the bartender, who won't leave me alone. She's already asked me if I'm an actor or a model about a hundred times. Normally, I'd be annoyed by this can't-take-a-hint flirting. But she provides good cover from what I'm actually doing here: lurking around my ex-girlfriend.

I turn my head as Eve steps closer to where I stand. Her dress makes her look like a mermaid; it's off the shoulder and tight down to her thighs before flaring out. I'm in awe of her; she accomplished everything she set out to do. In prison, I wished to see this moment. Here it is.

Eve's head moves around as her eyes scan the room. Absentmindedly, I rub my chest, feeling my body sway toward her like a magnet. There's a part of me waiting to see her flinch or show an emotion, as though maybe, on some level, she notices my presence.

She smiles. God, but I missed seeing this. Watching her happiness makes me feel straight up euphoric. Following her gaze, I freeze. Her eyes are locked on a clean-cut preppy boy who is half my size. Calm settles into her demeanor. My fists automatically clench as my body registers fury—*she's mine*. I move up to my toes in anger before settling myself back down.

He takes her in his arms. Holy fuck, seeing this hurts like hell. I knew the guy existed, but nothing could prepare me for watching my woman in the arms of another man. They're chatting and I take a minute to inspect this asshole.

He's sporting a navy tux that fits him too well to be rented. A white-gold Rolex Daytona watch—the same one my father wears—sits on his wrist. His hair is clean cut, his face shaven. *Is this Eve's type now?*

An old man with stark-white hair walks over to the happy couple interrupting their conversation. That boyfriend of hers stands slightly behind her, dutifully. I want to stride over and punch his lights out. Instead, I take another deep pull of my drink before grinding my teeth together.

6

EVE

"Eve!" Cyrus Nazarian walks up to me wearing a perfectly fitted black suit complete with a pink silk tie and matching pocket square. After immigrating from Iran without a dollar to his name, he worked from the ground up to become one of the largest real estate investors in L.A. Just like me, he gives back.

We kiss each other twice, once on both cheeks. As I've learned since living here, this is the typical Persian greeting. "I still can't believe the new wing," he exclaims. "I wonder if the donor is here tonight."

"No idea," I shrug. "Whoever he is though, he just changed life for these kids."

A few months ago, during a tutor meeting at the Kids Learning Club, the president let us know about an anonymous donor who handed over a forkful of cash without any demands in return.

"I doubt he's from around here," he whispers conspiratorially.

"Yeah? Why do you say that?"

"People in L.A. want their name up on everything. If they give a penny to even a remotely decent cause, they want public credit for it."

He lifts his glass to me. I have to admit, he has a good point. "You look drop-dead gorgeous, by the way. I'll see you next week."

I turn my head around and feel my skin prickle as if I'm being watched. I shake the feeling off; seeing Vincent has clearly put me on the crazy train. Marshall steps beside me, a reminder that while Vincent is in my city, nothing has changed. I'm here at a charity event with my sweet boyfriend. He's annoying me with his presence, but still, I'm safe.

I move around the bar area with Marshall by my side, shifting my hands to my thighs to lift up my gown so I can walk easier. I can feel the eyes of the expensive crowd watch me, but it only makes me raise my head higher.

Marshall's hands gently graze my lower back and I flinch from his touch. He knows how to play the part of devoted boyfriend, but tonight, he's making my skin crawl.

I clear my throat, wanting to change my train of thought. "Have you started the book I gave you?"

Last week, I lent him *The Autobiography of Malcolm X as told to Alex Haley*, by Malcolm X. Time Magazine recommended it as one of the most important nonfiction books of the twentieth century. And on top of that, it still reigns as one of the most important books in my life.

"Nah. Not sure I'll read it," he says with a quiet chuckle.

"But—"

"You know how busy I am." He squints his eyes, confused. It's not like me to push him. Everything we do is easy and relaxed.

Memories of Vincent and me discussing this exact book over dinner pop into my head. I push Marshall's dirty-blond hair away from his eyes, reminding myself that any woman would be lucky to be with a man like him. Who cares if he shares my passion for reading?

He pulls me into a soft embrace, careful not to grab too hard when he notices my sad demeanor. "Eve. You okay?"

I force a smile, but it comes out as a grimace.

"Hey," he lowers his brows, concerned. "You look upset. If you really want me to read the book—"

"No, no. I'm fine. Just a tough day at work."

"Those guys giving you a hard time?" He pats my back. "Just hang in there. Soon you'll make partner like you've always wanted. Just a few more years of the suck."

"Yeah," I reply miserably, wishing he'd say something more along the lines of 'If they fuck with you again, I'll beat their asses.' But that's just my inner Blue-House girl talking, as opposed to the respectable new me. He knows how poorly they treat me, but agrees that with enough work and dedication, I'll be able to show myself apart from the others.

Marshall orders me a glass of Sancerre from the bartender who thankfully, pours quickly. Only yesterday, I loved how easy and simple my life was with Marshall. And now, everything I thought was working is turned upside down. Maybe I ought to just try harder. A nagging voice inside my head tells me that I may as well just start fresh with another man. Why hang onto someone I don't really like? But a more mature voice chimes in, telling me I've got something good and I ought to do the mature thing and stick it out. Relationships take work. If I just open up more, maybe what we have can be *more*.

I never let him know what the Learning Club means to me and that it's not just a side gig. Sure, I've told him that I was raised in a pretty shitty part of New York City and that helping kids with potential, but limited means, is both fulfilling and necessary. But I never talked to him about my history. The result is that a huge chunk of who I am, or who I was, has been deleted. Up until today, I loved that fact.

No—I still love that fact. And I'm going to prove it to myself right now. I place my glass of wine back on the bar and squeeze his hand. "Let's get out of here," I step closer to him, an invitation in my eyes. First, I need to get my physical body on track. And then, we can talk.

"Hell yes," he smiles wide. "My place or yours?"

"Mine."

Draping an easy arm around my shoulders, we walk across the room and leave the event.

Questions and reservations knock on my head again. I take a deep swallow, telling my thoughts to shut it. Plenty of people begin relationships without digging up and sharing their old dirt. He knows the me of today, and he likes it. The rest will follow. I seal my will, determined to make a last-ditch effort. My agonizing is nothing but stress from seeing Vincent. Marshall is great. We're great. Everything is great!

We step into the car, but before we can buckle up, I grab him by the lapels and press my lips against his. I'm dying to feel that connection, and I desperately want to remember that what Marshall offers is good for me. Waiting to hook up until we reach my apartment is no longer an option. I need reassurance—now.

The minute we touch, my body recognizes his clean scent and gently melts. He's a good kisser, with soft but firm lips. Gently caressing my back, I urge him on by kissing him deeper, pushing for more. I want to want this—so badly. I let out a groan, hoping the sound will jumpstart my body.

"Eve, oh—" he murmurs.

I grab him harder, "Tell me." I pull my dress up to my thighs to spread my legs, straddling him and grinding down. I squeeze my internal muscles on a mission to get my body on board with this moment. "Tell me what you want. I'll do anything," I beg between dry kisses. I need him to make me forget.

7

VINCENT

I walk out of the event a few minutes after Eve leaves when I immediately spot her prissy boyfriend stepping into her car; it turns on but doesn't move. I get closer before wishing I hadn't. I can see through the window that her boyfriend is all. Fucking. Over. Her.

My body lunges forward, wanting to rip the car door open and beat his ass—jealous energy coursing through my veins. I gather myself by taking deep inhales through my mouth and exhaling through my nose. The result is a sound more animal than human. But the idea of another man kissing her perfect lips. Touching her full breasts. Listening to her moans.

"She's mine!" I roar, turning from the scene and cursing.

Sweat beads on my forehead. Does he make her feel good? The thought of her enjoying what another man can do is enough to make me sick. I kick the ground, small rocks flying ahead of me. I want to break something.

I drop down to the curb, unable to stand. Eve may be the love of my life, but the truth is that as of now, I have no hold over her. She can be with whomever she wants, whenever she wants. And it's all my fault. One thing's for damn sure: I've gotta make this right between us and get her back.

I pick up my phone, ordering a car to bring me to her apartment building. If I have to wait all fucking night and day for her to show up, I'll do it. I don't give a fuck if she comes home at three in the morning with mascara smeared on her face from a late night with this asshole—or a smile and a coffee in her hands in the morning. I'll take Eve any way I can get her.

8

EVE

I'm in the process of unbuttoning his shirt when I feel his hands at my shoulders, pushing me back. "Wow, let's relax a second."

His blue eyes are startled. "Huh?" I pant, confused.

"What's gotten into you?" His mouth is parted and eyes drawn to slits. He's mad.

Embarrassment blazes through me as I think of how to explain myself. "Well, I just thought—"

Before I can finish speaking, his hands spread beneath my ass. I'm lifted off his lap and into the driver's seat. "What if we were seen?" He straightens his skinny black tie. "I mean, a kiss is one thing. But what you tried to do is an entirely other—"

"Are you kidding me right now?" I start to fix my dress as my body turns cold. It's as though the temperature between us has dropped twenty degrees.

"This isn't even about me, Eve," he exclaims, throwing his hands up in the air. "It's about you. People know your car." He turns his head to look out the window and shakes his head in disapproval. "What would they think? You're not a college girl. You're a world-known attorney for God's sake." He slicks his hair as I unroll my gown down my thighs.

Our car ride back to his upscale apartment complex is full of awkward silence. I pull up to his front door, exhausted and reeling from Vincent. Having Marshall near me is only making things worse.

"Sweetie, let's talk a second." His voice is quiet. Unbuckling his belt and leaning toward me, I raise my hands in front of my face, as if to say, don't get any closer.

"You know what? I think we're done." The minute the words leave my lips, I feel a rush of relief.

His head rears back, shock moving across his features. "What are you talking about? Done with what?"

"It's just not working between us. I've got too much happening at my office. And this isn't feeling good to me anymore." I shrug, realizing this is all coming out of left field to him. Hell, it's coming out of the woodwork for me too, but I don't want to try harder with him. I need to find someone else. Someone different.

"Because I didn't want to screw you in public?" he spits out his words furiously.

I do my best not to roll my eyes; it's not as if we ever said we loved each other. We were dating out of convenience. "No. It's not that. It's because what we had was nothing more than easy. And I'm just not happy anymore." I bring my gaze to his face, staring at him directly so he knows I'm serious. The truth hurts and no one knows that better than me. But in my opinion, it's better to rip off the Band-Aid than send someone off with a lie.

He waits expectantly for me to fight back or to show emotion, but I have none.

"I was wife'ing you up," he yells, throwing the door open before jumping out of my car. The side door swings open next as he grabs his neatly folded jacket from the back seat. "You're a cold bitch, you know that?" And with those parting words, the door slams with a *bang*.

My fingers grip the steering wheel, knowing in my gut that what he said is true. I'm not warm and soft—not anymore. Maybe I'm just meant to be alone, forever.

Shifting the car in gear, I get to my building in record time. Pulling into the parking lot, I jump out of my car and run as fast as my high heels will take me to the elevator. I just want to take off my shoes, wash my face, eat a bowl of cereal, and pass out. Sliding my keys into my apartment door, I pause. I can feel a body behind me. My old instincts immediately kick in as I turn, lifting my keys in my hand like a weapon.

He looms in front of me like a dark shadow.

"V-Vincent?"

I take a step back.

He steps closer. "I've been trying to call you the last few months, but you never answered." His voice is deep and low. All I can do is blink as he leans his huge body against the doorframe. "Why don't you invite me in? We should talk, Eve. It's been a while, yeah?"

I finally look him up and down as a lump rises in my throat. He looks like danger in a black tux—muscled thighs covered in a pair of tapered black pants and a wide chest encased in a crisp white tuxedo shirt. I crane my neck to look up at his face. God, he's *gorgeous*.

I lean my weight onto my right leg and lift my chin, needing to get a grip on reality. "No." The word flies out of my mouth like a whip. My feelings are all across the map, and I can't get a hold of them. I move to my safe default: bitch mode.

"No?" He looks at me incredulously, crossing his huge arms in front of his chest.

"I'm not a kid anymore, Vincent." I swallow. "You can't just boss me around. I have plans for myself and they don't include you. Now, if you'll go back to your hotel or wherever you're staying, you can send me an email and we can find a good time to talk. I assume this is work related, right?" My voice comes out as high and mighty, but I've got to harden myself as much as I can around this man if I want to keep myself straight.

"Let's talk for a minute. Touch base." He squints, and I can see the slight formation of crow's feet at the corner of his eyes. Vincent is a man now.

I do my best to stay composed, but I'm grasping on every strand of my self-worth to keep from crumbling. "Who the hell do you think you are, Vincent? You left me seven years ago after ripping my heart to shreds and forcing me out of the only city I ever knew, after feeding me to the dogs, no less." I throw my hands up in the air. "I'm not a teenager anymore. You can't just—come here!" I slam my foot onto the ground, angry and hurting so badly. I bite my lip, even more upset when I see the pity cross his face.

He stares at me, remorse coating the darkness of his eyes. We're silent, but my heart pounds a mile a minute. Can he hear it?

Lifting his heavy arms, he links his hands behind his neck before dropping them back down to his side. "Eve," he starts, licking his lips. "I know you've grown up, and I'm glad for that. You've achieved your goals and you're astounding." He lowers his voice and I strain my ears, subconsciously trying to hear every word.

My body, on its own accord, leans toward him. "You are allowed to be angry, but I hoped we could talk tonight. I know you aren't a teenager anymore, okay? We've both grown. I didn't mean to piss you off by coming to your work. But in my defense, I tried to call you. You wouldn't answer." He touches the edge of my face so gently—I have to wonder if it happened or if I was hallucinating.

I clear my throat. I should pull off my heel and stab him in the stomach. Call the cops, maybe. But I don't want to show him just how angry I am. He shouldn't know how much he affects me. I refuse to let him know.

I focus on small mundane things because the large issues are too much to handle. "You don't shave anymore?"

A lazy grin spreads across his mouth. We're barely a few inches apart now, and I can smell him, woodsy and clean.

"You know I don't like to shave when I don't have to," he whispers. "And you keep your hair back tight or straight, but I know that after you wash it, it's long and curly." His nostrils flare as his eyes move down to my lips and back up again. I keep my eyes focused, not giving in. Still I notice how huge he is. Thick arms. Wide chest.

My face instantly flushes—I need to change the subject. "You're making it out west like you wanted."

"Yes. And you became a lawyer. You graduated early from Stanford, magna cum laude. You finished second in your law school class. Janelle has her own salon—"

"Wait, what?" It's as if the music just stopped. I ball my hands into fists as I'm snapped back to reality. "You've been keeping tabs on me?" I take a step away from him, feeling violated. Vincent has been watching me for years. He ruined my life, and what, did he stick around to watch my unraveling?

He squints his eyes again and slightly tilts his head as if he's confused.

"I'm not yours to watch, Vincent." His name flies out of my mouth like a whip. "So, I should assume you know the hell I went through after you ruined my life?"

Honestly, I can't believe how much rage I have inside me right now. It's bubbling up and I feel the sudden urge to slap him across the face. I may have told myself that my hatred and resentment disappeared and that I grew up and out of the pain he caused, but clearly, it was only lying dormant.

His face flashes hot with his own anger. "For fuck's sake, Eve. I did the best I could to protect you. And that part of my life is over now." I watch him clench his jaw.

"Protect me? By cheating on me and making me believe we had a- a future?" I stutter before letting out an ironic laugh. "No. I'm not letting you in." I look him up and down, registering his clothes. "And why are you wearing a tux?" I drop my hands to my hips, the thought momentarily stunning me that Vincent may have been at the gala tonight, watching me.

He smiles with that faraway look in his eyes; I recognize it as the one he makes when an idea is taking shape in his head. "Let's rock-paper-scissors. If I win, you let me in. If you win, I leave."

"You're kidding." This man is infuriating. He thinks he can just change the subject? "This isn't a game. This is my life," I exclaim.

One of my neighbors, an older woman in her seventies, pokes her head out her door. "Keep it down!" she shouts angrily.

I want to point at Vincent—tell her it's all his fault. Instead, I attempt to channel a civilized person. "Everything is fine," I smile tightly. "My apologies."

"Well, it's after eleven and I'm doing a commercial tomorrow!" She slams the door and I look back at Vincent. Chuckling, he reaches out his hand. "Come on. Let's play."

Tears prick my eyes. I'm proud of him, but it also hurts. His dream was also mine, once. We were supposed to be about truth and honesty, but in the end, he gutted me. If he thinks he can bring out the old me with a stupid game we used to play, he's mistaken. That girl was burned alive years ago and there's no trace left of her.

He stands tall, his stance almost playful.

"Okay. Fine. On three. But if I win, you're gone, right?"

He smiles. I'll call him on it if I think he cheated.

I put out my hand reluctantly. "Rock-paper-scissors says shoot!" My fingers morph into a fist to make rock, and of course, the asshole's hand comes out straight to make paper. He wins.

I open and close my mouth like a dead fish, wanting to find fault. Instead, I open my front door. Pulling off my heels, I leave them by the door before walking barefoot to my kitchen table.

"Prison," I say point blank, taking a seat. Vincent sits in front of me, his long legs stretching out below the table. I cross mine, making sure not to accidentally brush against his.

"Yes. I got out six months ago, but had to stay in New York for probation. The last seven years have been dedicated to the Milestone. I worked my ass off in lockup and continued the work after I got out. And now I'm finally there, out in Nevada and living on the rez."

"And how's your father?" I press my lips together firmly, trying to compose my trembling body.

"You cut to the chase now, yeah? No more running and hiding?" His lips quirk in a grin.

I smile back sarcastically. "Nope. Those days are done and gone, Vincent."

"Though nothing can bring back the hour of splendor in the grass, of glory in the flower..." He pauses, waiting for me to finish the poem.

"I'm not here to quote Wordsworth," I exclaim, "Jesus." I shake my head angrily, but my heart flutters; he knows I love poetry. And of course, he's quoting from "Splendor in the Grass," a poem that speaks of childhood as a time when we're the most able to see clearly, before adulthood comes and jades us. But that's the thing about adulthood —we can't escape the loss of innocence. Our bodies change, but so do our minds.

He laughs, shrugging his massive shoulders. "What can I tell you? I did a lot of reading in prison."

I cross my arms over my chest, giving him my best I'm-a-lawyer-and-I'll-nail-your-balls-to-the-wall glare. There's no way in hell I'm letting him sweet-talk me right now.

"Okay, okay!" He lifts his arms up in front of him like a shield. "We're business partners in the Mile. The family is silent, of course. Aside from that, we've got nothing else between us. I've separated."

"Separated?" I ask inquisitively. "How did you manage that?" I shake my head in disbelief.

"Well," he sighs. "I guess when I met you, I started doubting the family. But I figured I made my bed and had no choice but to sleep in it. My senior year of college, when we were together" —he says, gesturing between us— "I thought it would be possible to keep one foot in and one foot out. I figured once I left New York, I'd be able to have the freedom."

I lean forward in my chair, wanting to look disgusted and angry over his mention of that time. Instead, I listen with bated breath.

"But in prison," he says, clearing his throat. "Shit started unraveling within the family. They got involved with things that I wouldn't stand behind. I was growing the Milestone and knew that I wanted no part of the family anymore. Told my father he could kill me if he wants. Or, he can let me run the business and we can be partners. But the Borignone table isn't mine to sit at anymore. Don't want that shit. And truthfully, you and I both know that I never did."

My jaw practically hits the floor with his utterly honest confession. His head stays raised, exuding strength. "I'm secure now, doing what I want."

I shift in my seat, my eyes darting to the floor. This is his lifelong dream he's about to live. I want to ask him if he remembers our first conversation over dinner the night we met. About changing one's path, and now, here we are—changed. But have we, really?

I clasp my hands together, gathering my wits. "Look, Vincent—"

"You sure do like to say my name a lot, Eve." Again, that roguish grin.

I blow air from my lips, exasperated. "Look," I repeat. "You can tell me anything you want. But let me get one thing straight." I lift a finger in the air. "Firstly, I have built a life here."

He looks around the apartment as if he's calling bullshit. My blood grows hot. How dare he judge me! Skimming my open floor plan, all of my furniture is modern and useful in clean beiges and soft browns. I'm just not a warm type, and I guess my apartment shows that. But that doesn't mean I'm not happy. Anyway, since when do throw pillows and blankets mean happy home? I own this place and I'm proud of that.

My hands grip the edge of my chair. "If you want to work with my firm right now, that's fine. But our relationship will be strictly business. You don't know me anymore, and I don't know you. And all those promises we made when we were kids are just that, promises made between kids. They don't matter. Your business is important to me—to the firm. So, I can make this work if you can." I shut my mouth and wait for his agreement.

He hums his assent calmly. "I understand the way I left all those years ago was..." he pauses, not finishing his sentence. "But for the sake of our dealings, I agree we must keep ourselves as strictly business. Actually" —he leans forward in his chair— "that's why I'm here. Your office is widely known as the best, and I need you for the Milestone."

My stomach sinks with his agreement, but I don't show it. I guess what else did I expect? That he'd come here and beg forgiveness?

"Well," I clear my throat. "I am good at what I do." I sit taller, doing my best to act as if I'm completely unaffected.

He shifts toward me, and I try not to swoon from how good he smells. "I like your gown. But you should have the straps tightened. They keep falling." His fingers graze against my bare skin as he lifts both straps back up my shoulders. My entire body freezes before melting from his touch.

He gets up to go and I stand up after him. We're facing each other and I internally groan, wishing I didn't take off my shoes earlier. My eyes dart to his feet; he's wearing a pair of steel-toed black boots, completely at odds with the tux. It doesn't match the outfit, but he makes it look rugged and sexy. He's impossibly tall and imposing. I'm struck by how small I feel. Almost at his mercy, and all at once, a blast of lust shoots straight through my blood. I'm hot and wet. *For him.*

He smirks wickedly. "I'll see you at the office, then." And with those words, he walks out my door.

9

EVE

I step into the office building's elevator with a grande coffee from Starbucks in my left hand and my Chanel purse slung over my right shoulder. It's Monday morning, and I'm wearing my extra-large and round black Dior sunglasses to hide the bags under my eyes; even my heaviest-duty concealer couldn't cover my dark circles today. Now that Vincent has reappeared, all I can do is agonize over every possible scenario in my head.

Thankfully, Marshall only called twice; his begging did nothing but turn me off even more, making it deadly clear that we are absolutely done.

The elevator door *dings* and I walk out into the hallway. I push through the firm's front doors expecting the hum of cold air conditioning to greet me. Instead, I feel as if I've just walked into an alternate universe.

The office is buzzing with noise. Instead of sitting in their respective cubicles, everyone is congregating at reception. Lauren is perched on top of the front desk, long legs crossed and dangling off the edge while Max, the young office tech guy, is giving her fuck-me eyes. The mergers and acquisitions group laughs together off to the right, clapping their hands in glee.

"Um, what the hell is going on here?" I push my sunglasses up on top of my head as my gaze works the room. "Did I miss something?"

Lauren's smile is joyous. "Oh. My. God, Eve! Vincent emailed the contract early this morning. He's already sent a four-million-dollar retainer, and this is just the beginning. The entire firm is trying to angle their way to work on the Milestone to get a cut of billable hours. Isn't this exciting? The best part is, the bosses are out celebrating together over a breakfast meeting, and they'll probably be out today golfing! Do you think bonuses will be larger this year?"

I roll my eyes. "I guess while the cat's away, the mice will play," I say quietly under my breath. I don't have the energy to get caught up in the party, and there's a ton of work on my desk I should be getting to. I walk as quickly as I can toward my office, but stop short when I see the DBC opening up beers in the conference room. They have their bottles raised high, about to cheers. Before they can notice my presence, I run into my office, slamming the door shut behind me.

The day passes quickly as I work on finalizing the details for a huge condominium closing I've got with the bank on Friday. I'm back and forth with the seller's attorney, haggling over contractual language. After filling out the last of the forms, I realize how badly I need to pee.

I get up, straighten my skirt, and head to the ladies' room. Luckily, the office has calmed down a bit as most people have already left. When I'm about to wash my hands, Lauren steps inside.

"There you are! I've tried to reach you all day. How was the gala?"

"Oh, it was fine. Broke up with Marshall." My voice is nonchalant.

"What?" she practically screams.

I shrug my shoulder before turning the water on.

"Is that why you're locked up in your office instead of celebrating?"

"No way." I shake my head. "You know I never really liked him," I reply, resigned.

"Well, everyone has been in the best mood. You should be, too." She sounds annoyed.

"I have a closing this week, and I had to finalize everything. My client wanted me to push for a lower purchase price before closing, and I wasn't happy with the contract language, so I had to negotiate the hell out of the sellers." I dry my hands on a paper towel before pulling the clip out of my hair and twisting it back up again.

"Tell me you're coming out with us to celebrate. Jonathan is already at the bar. I was just about to barge into your office after I finished freshening up." She drenches her hair with texturizing spray and fluffs up the roots with her fingertips.

I open my mouth ready to tell her that there is no way in hell I'm going out tonight. But before I can start, she pushes her bottle into my hand.

"Please use some for tonight. Your hair is super limp and you need va-voom if you're going to pick any guys with me after the douchebags leave."

Ah, there it is; she needs a wingman. I want to laugh, but all I have the energy for right now is a half smile. "I don't think so. What I really need is a long hot shower and dinner. I would be terrible tonight, anyway. I mean, look at me." I gesture to my rumpled appearance.

She pouts in an over-exaggerated way. "First of all, you're gorgeous even when tired. And second of all, Vincent put in a contractual request that guarantees you work on the project." Her high voice turns to pleading. "You need to be celebrating like crazy right now. You're like, the woman of the freakin' hour. No—the woman of the year." She claps.

I frown.

She huffs, exasperated. "I'm not sure why you look so pissed off. By the way, you're going to wrinkle if you keep making that face. Don't say I didn't warn you when you've got lines in your forehead that even Millennial Plastic Surgery can't get rid of."

Now it's my turn to roll my eyes.

"Eve," she says emphatically, holding me by the shoulders.

"Imagine the hours you're going to bill. Not least, Vincent is insanely sexy. I was dreaming of him last night. I wonder how his beard would feel rubbing against my thighs."

"Oh, come on, Lauren. He's a client." Her comment has my heart squeezing.

"Well, I'm not his attorney. Unlike you, I don't have any obligation to keep a distance." She moves her eyebrows up and down like she can't wait to get down and dirty with him. It's as if I can't breathe.

"Anyway, I tried to Google him, but the man has like, zero social media presence. So annoying. Who in this day and age is this impossible to find?"

What I want to tell her is she's absolutely correct. Vincent is, for all intents and purposes, virtually nonexistent; I know this for a fact because I looked him up myself, hoping maybe I would see his new life since he got out of prison. For a guy who used to have thousands of followers on social media, it's crazy how he was able to just erase that entire part of his life. Unfortunately, I even found myself snooping on Daniela—something I haven't done since I left New York City. I was pleasantly surprised to learn that she was busted for cocaine possession and sent directly to a rehab facility. After a six-month stint, she went to Colombia to help in her father's business. I tried to find out more, but she too seems to have vanished from the social-media stratosphere.

Lauren looks at me happily as though she's waiting for me to joke about Vincent's hotness or illusiveness, but I can't chat with her about Vincent. I can barely think about him when I'm all alone, for God's sake.

"You look like you're having an entire conversation in your head right now. What's wrong, babe? Come on, let's go out and have fun," she begs. "A drink or five will do you good."

I grimace. "But—"

She raises a hand, cutting me off. "Women stick together, right? Don't leave me alone with those savages."

"You sure you want to call in the girl card tonight?"

"If I use it, will you come? Because I look really good tonight and I don't want it to go to waste," she pouts.

I laugh. "Fine. Let me get my bag."

"Yay!" She sprays my hair quickly before dropping the can back into her purse and links her arm into mine. Clinging to me like a barnacle, she ensures I don't duck and run as we walk back into my office.

"Maybe a drink is in order, even if it's with the DBC."

"That's my girl!" she says with glee as I take my bag from underneath my desk before fluffing my own roots. I sling my purse over my shoulder, ready for a break.

"Let's just go get this over with."

She leads me out the front doors and into the elevator.

Luckily, we don't have to walk too far to the bar since it's only a few blocks from the office.

The entire place is packed with suits. Moving toward the back, we find Jonathan and the DBC sitting together at a long wooden table in the corner. They shift over grudgingly to make space for us. Jeff pushes an open Corona Light in my direction and I grab it and bring it to my lips, not pausing before taking a long gulp.

"Thirsty?" He chuckles. I ignore him. The truth is, the ice-cold beer is seriously hitting the spot right now.

I turn to Lauren, who's staring at the menu. "Are we ordering any food? I'm starved."

Jonathan puts his hand up to call the waitress over. When she gets to our table, he orders three baskets of fries, an assortment of cheeses, two orders of beef sliders, and shots of tequila for everyone. The liquor choice is a pretty aggressive move for a Monday, even for Jonathan.

He takes a nice long look at the waitress's ass before turning back to me. "Who would have thought you, of all people, would bring in our biggest client to date? You're a brilliant girl, Eve. I don't tell you enough." Even though it's backhanded, I still smile from the compliment and take another gulp of my beer, hoping the bottle covers the blush that has taken over my face.

The drinks arrive. We all bring our shot glasses up in the air, ready to toast the Milestone when the table goes quiet. Everyone's heads crane up. I swivel my head to look where they're staring. The moment I see who's coming, I gasp, startled by the huge, hulking form walking toward me.

My eyes greedily travel over every inch of him. He's wearing dark denim and a gray button-down shirt. His hair is incredibly mussed, as if he recently put his hands through it. If Janelle were here, she'd say he looks like he just fucked the shit out of someone. I swallow hard. *Vincent.* My heart pounds his name, almost painfully. *What is he even doing here?*

Jonathan stands to welcome him. I glance around the table, noticing that no one else looks surprised. Plastering a fake smile on my face, I do my best to act like nothing is amiss.

"So glad you were able to make it out tonight." Jonathan takes Vincent's hand in a firm shake. "I wasn't sure if you'd be able to find the time," Jonathan exclaims. "Come and sit down. Oh, Eve, scoot over."

I move myself to the left as Vincent sits down to my right. He angles his body toward me and puts out his hand for a cordial hello. I shake it calmly without making any eye contact before glancing around to make sure no one sees our handshake as anything more than strictly business. I finally look up at his piercing gaze.

Before I can cross my legs, his denim-clad leg presses against my bare thigh. I'm taken aback for a moment, silently cursing myself for wearing a skirt today. Sure, it's appropriate work attire since the length hits mid-knee. But sitting down, it has ridden up and left most of my legs exposed. I'd be lying if I said the contact didn't heat me up inside, but it also makes me vulnerable. I can't have any skin-on-skin with this man if I want to keep my sanity. *Business. Everything with Vincent is now strictly business.*

Jonathan pipes up, immediately garnering Vincent's attention. "We're going to be spending a lot of time together. I'm glad you came out tonight." Jonathan lifts his drink to cheers, and Vincent responds with a nod. I shoot back my drink in one swallow, ignoring the fact that I've barely eaten all day.

The truth is, I shouldn't be surprised that Vincent is here. Jonathan always aims to be friends with clients, and a few nights a month, he expects us to come out and schmooze. It not only buys us leniency if there are delays, but it also makes for an easier work environment when we're all friendly.

"Eve just arrived, too. This girl can outwork anyone else. She's the perfect person for the work you've got, and I must say, you were absolutely right to request her." Jonathan's face is turning red from drinking, but it's clear that he's in his comfort zone.

"So, Jonathan." Vincent clears his throat and the entire table quiets, seemingly waiting for his next word. "I think it's important for her to see the Milestone."

"Yes. I was planning to email Eve tomorrow morning to let her know that she should head over to Nevada right away. She'll be able to do lots of due diligence on the project; she's already read the files you sent over prior to our meeting. It's all good. How long do you think she'll need?" His voice is all excitement. I feel shell-shocked, as though his words are bombs.

"I think a week would be sufficient for this first trip," Vincent replies casually.

"A week?" I shout, practically leaping out of my chair. My eyes immediately move around the table; everyone stares at me as if I've lost my mind. "Oh..." I smile, letting out a small self-conscious laugh and tucking a stray hair behind my ear. "I don't think a week is really necessary. I mean, I could do it in two or three days. I'm sure. Or one day, even."

Jonathan's mouth spreads in a wide grin, but behind his eyes, he's telling me he will cut me if I anger our client. "Yes, it's true Eve, you are a fast worker." He laughs, trying to ease the awkwardness. "But if Vincent thinks a week is necessary, I'm sure a week is what you'll need."

Jonathan cranes his head looking around for the waitress. Unable to find her, he turns to me with a request on his lips. "Eve, the waitress is so damn slow. Why don't you go to the bar and find out if the drinks and food are coming soon? Vincent, what do you want? Eve will order for you while she's up there."

I make a move to stand when Vincent's heavy hand grips my bare thigh locking me down in place. It's huge and hot and incredibly strong; there is no escape. Without any preamble, warmth travels straight into my belly and down through my legs, the strength of which I haven't felt in ages.

Vincent turns back to Jonathan, his voice short. "Why don't you just flag down the waitress? Eve doesn't need to get up."

Jonathan's mouth snaps shut as his nostrils flare. I don't need Vincent to be my champion. If he keeps this up, everyone is going to assume what we have between us. And they'd be thrilled to spread a rumor that the reason I got this job is because I spread my legs. I hate the fact that I have to think this way, but what else can I do? I'm in this position and it forces me to keep all my hackles up.

I need to do damage control before anyone gets the wrong idea. "It's no big deal. Let me go check on it; it's my pleasure." Vincent's hand squeezes on my thigh again, a little higher this time and I swallow, my throat running dryer than the Sahara.

I tell my body to relax, but my mind wanders to what those hands can do. I flush, the heat moving up my collarbone and into my face. I'm powerless. Once my mind gets the memo, I relax into his grip.

Luckily, the conversation turns moot as the waitress shows up with a huge tray filled with more drinks and food. The moment she places everything out on the table, he lifts his hand from my leg; I want to say I feel relief, but I don't. Instead, it feels like loss.

Vincent looks up at the waitress, his body language casual. "I'll have a Blue Label on the rocks, please." The waitress smiles seductively, eyes noticeably widening as she checks him out.

What's he going to do? Will he flirt back? I mean, he's a gorgeous single man. Wait. Is he single? Maybe he isn't. He probably isn't. Not that I care.

He turns his head to dismiss her, and I quickly look to Lauren as

if I'm about to tell her something enormously important, hoping he
didn't catch me staring.

It only takes a few minutes for the waitress to return with his
drink. I watch him from my side-eye as he picks it up with his right
hand, bringing the clear glass full of ice and amber liquid to his full
lips which are more sensuous than any man's has a right to be. Tilting
his head back slightly, the drink goes straight down his throat.

"So, Vincent, where are you originally from?" Jeff sits up eagerly,
hoping to make conversation. Now that the asshole knows the work is
ours, he'll probably try to angle himself to get involved and get a cut
of billable hours. What an asshole.

"New York," Vincent replies, clipped.

"Born and raised in California," he smiles. "Eve is from New York,
too. Aren't you?" He looks between us questioningly, as if it's oddly
coincidental we're both from the same state.

"Yes, I am." I try to keep my voice even as if there's nothing I'm
hiding.

Jeff continues, his sharp eyes focusing on Vincent. "What part? I
have family in Great Neck."

"Oh?" Vincent stares at him dead on and Jeff immediately cowers,
his pupils widening in anxiety. I have to admit, between the tatts, the
scruff, and the muscles, Vincent is intimidating. Add in his death
stare and he's got all the ingredients for how-to-be-scary-as-hell. But
it's not just his physical traits that make him so intimidating. It's more
than that.

Vincent moves his body as if to say: this is me—I dress, walk, and
act, as I truly am; if you don't like it, you can go fuck yourself.

Vincent turns to Lauren as she asks him how long he's staying out
here in L.A. His reply is muffled, but she giggles. Making eye contact
with the waitress, I lift my beer and put up a finger, miming "one
more please." Luckily, she nods in understanding.

"You should hang out with me and Eve tonight. We're celebrating." Lauren's eyes sparkle.

"Oh yeah?" He takes another gulp of his drink before looking
between us.

"Eve broke up with her boyfriend and I'm totally single. We're celebrating our freedom." She winks at me and my stomach drops.

After a polite smile, I face forward. Still I try, as shadily as possible, to hear every word of their conversation. Unfortunately, all my worries gather together, clamoring for headspace. *He ruined you once; he could do it again. The only thing you can count on anymore is your work.* Fucking emotions!

Thankfully, the waitress returns, handing me another drink. I wrap my hands around the cold bottle, ready to lift it to my lips when I realize I'm a few sips away from drunk. Water—I need water. I pick up my cup of tap and drink.

The conversation flows and Vincent looks totally relaxed. Everyone wants to impress him, but he maintains his laid-back and even-keeled demeanor. His calmness is *infuriating*. He obviously put our past behind him. Watching him act so calmly is making me realize there is only one truth: Vincent never cared about me. If he did, how could he possibly be so nonchalant right now? I need a break. On shaky legs, I manage to stand, albeit swaying a little bit first.

"I'm going to use the restroom; if you'll excuse me," I politely tell the table. I beeline to the bathroom, relieved to find it empty. After peeing quickly, I stand in front of the sink to wash my hands. But when I look up into the mirror, I realize I may cry. The last few years I've been unshakable. And now Vincent is back and I can already feel the tears welling. I bring my hands to my lips, puffy and red. I hardly recognize the woman staring back at me; I'm everything I wanted to become...yet more unfulfilled than ever. I feel ungrateful, confused, and stressed out. I have to leave.

I open the door, pausing as my eyes register what's in front of me. She's tall, with gorgeous red hair and a tight black dress. If this isn't a sign, I don't know what is. I'm about to lose it.

I do my best to politely say goodbye to the table, feigning a headache as an excuse and avoiding Vincent's prying eyes. I walk away with a casual wave, as if I'm in no real rush, but once I'm far enough out of sight, I run out the front door and cross the street. I need to create physical distance between me and my shitty coworkers, who treat me terribly but I'm too scared to report—and Vincent, the only man on earth with the ability to break me into pieces.

I use my arm to wipe my tears away before pulling out my phone and clicking on the Uber app. Glancing back to the bar, I see Vincent jump out the front door, his head swiveling from left to right as if he's searching. I hear him loudly curse before turning back inside. Leaning against the building, tears blur my vision. I just want to go home.

* * *

I get back into my apartment and pick up my phone to call Janelle. I haven't spoken to her in a week. I hit FaceTime on my phone, needing to see her. She answers after the third ring, her hair tied in a white towel-turban. She looks exhausted but happy from a long day and night at her salon. I know that no matter how tired her feet get from standing all day, she's fulfilled. Things aren't always easy, but neither she nor I have any doubt this is her life's calling.

"Hey, sissy!" She smiles, blue eyes shining. They dim as she assesses my state.

"You look drunk. Bad drunk."

"Yeah, you can say that," I swallow. "But there's more."

"How much more." There's a question in her voice.

"More more," I reply, dread webbing my insides.

"Talk," she says in that no-nonsense way of hers.

"Well," I start, pulling off my heels and planting myself comfortably on my bed. "Vincent's back."

She gasps.

I fill her in on all the details of the Milestone and how he's now *technically* a client of mine. When I get to the part of him showing up at my door after the Kids Learning Club gala, she looks downright furious.

"Jesus," she replies, her forehead crinkling. "What does he look like? I wanna get a good visual."

"He's physically rougher. Bigger, even. Tatts and dark scruff like he couldn't be bothered to shave. But I guess when he talks, he's still sort of the same. Brilliant. What he built out in Nevada is pretty unbelievable."

She purses her lips. "You've got a job to do, Eve. Don't let that piece-of-shit-dickhead-motherfucking-asshole come between you and your work." I can see the sneer on her face, but I'd bet money that she's got a finger pointing at me.

"He wrecked me. My entire life was thrown into chaos because of Vincent Borignone." I can feel a headache coming on along with a serious dose of anger.

"No shit."

"And now," I exclaim, standing up with the phone in front of me as I unzip and then shimmy out of my skirt. "He comes back and wants us to be normal. But how can I be normal? Is he insane?" I question angrily, unbuttoning my blouse before flinging it onto the floor.

"Listen, Eve. Do not let him steamroll over your life again. If you can't handle working with him, just pass him over. Either give him to one of those assholes you work with or tell your boss that it's dangerous to do business with him. You don't need this—"

"No," I reply quickly, cutting her off as I walk over to my dresser and pull out a pair of pajamas. "If I let his business go, he'll win. He's the biggest deal to come through my door and I'm not going to just back down."

"You know what? You're right," she shouts, pumping a fist in the air. "Anyway, he's the one who should be scared. Not you. Let me remind you: you did nothing the fuck wrong."

"Exactly. But, Janelle, what if he didn't actually—"

"Good, so it's settled," Janelle decrees. "Wash your face. Sleep. Tomorrow morning go for a run and drink your coffee. And when you get dressed, put your big-girl panties on because we are not letting him take even one more thing from you."

I nod my head in solidarity. "You're right."

"Of course, I am."

"I'm gonna sleep. My hangover tomorrow is going to suck."

"Take an Advil now."

I change into cozy sleep clothes, wash my face, and climb into bed. It only takes a moment for me to burst into tears; it's an assault. Salty water runs through my sinuses and floods my face like a torrential downpour. Whatever strength I had from my phone conversation is now nothing but dust.

I spend the rest of the night awake in my bed, feeling my emotions like waves as they come and go from the forefront of my mind. I want to block them, but it's not possible. As though I were a bystander in my own life, I replay the ending of Vincent and me, and my heart manages to break all over again.

10

EVE

It's been a week since the disastrous night at the bar, and now I'm sitting on Vincent's private plane on my way to Nevada to visit the Milestone. Per Jonathan's orders, I'm to complete due diligence that cannot be done remotely. I already spoke with Vincent's assistant, Kimber, to ready all the files.

This is my first flight since I came out to California. Once I got out here, I never left. Janelle asked me to come back to New York for Christmas and other holidays, but I always refused—too much pain and memories in my home city that I don't want to deal with. *Can't* deal with.

I let my fingers glide against the beautiful tan leather seat, the type of luxury poor-girl dreams are made of. The plane is so roomy and beautiful. Although I wanted to fly commercial, Kimber advised it would be easier to fly private as it would decrease my travel time. I was hesitant at first but ultimately agreed.

Staring out the window and watching us ascend, I grip the wooden armrests. With shaking hands, I put a piece of gum in my mouth, taking Janelle's advice so my ears don't pop. I shut my eyes and lean my head against the cushy seat, not letting myself think about the plane crashing. But the second my mind starts to run, I wish I had death on my mind, because all I can think about is Vincent and what will become of this trip.

The plane finally stabilizes and I open my eyes, slowly at first. Staring out the window, I'm in awe of the blue sky with nothing but the clouds below me.

Pulling out my laptop, I read about Nevada's history with the Tribe. Regardless of what is or isn't happening between Vincent and me, I've been paid to do a job and I'm nothing if not competent. I always stay on task, no matter what craziness is going on around me. This way, if things go belly up, I have my work to fall back on.

"Hello. I'm Alina, your stewardess for the flight. Are you comfortable?"

I hum out a "Yes," not looking up from my screen.

"Would you like a drink?" Her soft voice asks.

"Sure," I continue to stare at my monitor.

"Water? Orange juice? A cocktail perhaps?"

"Huh?" I look up at her, exasperated at the constant interruptions. My eyes lock on her face and I pause. She's gorgeous and tall, with long blonde hair and clear blue eyes. Her tight navy dress shows off her slight curves. Deep in my gut, I know this is Vincent's type. Or at least, I always figured this was the type of girl who suits him best. Model perfect. I immediately feel stung, wondering if he's been with her. I can just imagine the two of them on this plane, her listening to his every command. *I can get on my knees, Vincent. You want me to bend over like this, Vincent?* Bitch! Between these wide seats and the private bedroom in the back, he would have opportunities abounding.

She gives me a small smile, and I do my best not to glare. I want to strangle her.

"Non-carbonated water is fine, thank you," I reply, my voice curt. I watch as she glides to the back of the cabin, narrow hips swaying with each step.

I swallow hard, embarrassed by my rude behavior as well as angry at myself for even caring. This woman has done nothing wrong. Okay, so maybe Vincent fucked her a million times on this plane—it shouldn't mean anything to me. She comes back to my seat and hands me my drink with a courteous smile. I take it and blink back my emotion before facing the window.

My email *dings* letting me know I have a new message in my inbox; the Wi-Fi on the plane makes it incredibly easy to refocus on my tasks. I refresh my browser, seeing five new messages from Jonathan. He's forever working like crazy to keep his spot as partner.

After Jonathan's divorce, he told me of his utter relief not to have a wife annoying him any longer to come home for dinner or spend time with the kids. His words were, "I can finally work in peace."

Is this how I'm going to spend my life? Alone with my work, nothing but the work, so help me God?

The plane lands smoothly. I walk to the door, rolling my suitcase behind me and politely thanking Alina and the captain for the trip. I step outside into the sunlight, finding a huge guy with a buzz cut, black T-shirt, jeans, and heavy work boots watching me from the bottom of the steps. I drop my sunglasses over my eyes and pop a fresh piece of gum into my mouth as I take the stairs from the plane's door onto the tarmac. He immediately grabs my bags as he leads the way to an extra-long black Escalade. As he places my things in the trunk, I make myself comfortable in the plush black leather seat.

He finally gets into the car, sitting in the chair next to mine. "Hey Mark, we're ready to go." His voice is deep.

The car begins to drive. "Welcome to Nevada. You must be thirsty." Pulling out a bottle of water from a cooler on the floor, he hands me one. Before I can take it out of his grip, we make eye contact—it's almost like a standoff. "So, you're Eve, huh?" His green eyes squint like he knows exactly who I am. I'm momentarily surprised, wondering what he's heard.

I raise my eyebrows, pursing my lips as I pull the water away from him. "Yes. And you are?" I look him up and down, noticing his body is corded with heavy muscle and his arms are sleeved with colorful ink. I can only imagine Lauren right now; she'd be going insane over him.

"Slade," he says, introducing himself. "I head security for the

Milestone." A small smirk forms his lips, but it's clear he isn't hitting on me. An alarm rings in my head: who is this man to Vincent? I gather my wits and get into questioning mode.

"So, where did you work before this?" I cross my legs and type out a quick message to Lauren about landing, trying to act as if I'm making casual conversation and don't care too much about his response. Meanwhile, I'm on complete alert, waiting to hear what he says so I can accurately gauge who he is in Vincent's life.

"I was in the Navy. Came home and met Vincent at the gym. The rest is history," he replies, not unkindly.

I tilt my head to the side, wondering if he's Borignone muscle. "Well, you must know him and his family." I'm watching his face intently to see if he understands my implication.

His body stiffens before letting out a quick laugh. "I know you've got lots of grit. But let's get one thing straight. I'm not here to hurt you. In fact, it's the opposite. While you're here, if there's anything you need, don't hesitate to ask me." He pulls out a card from the pocket in the seat in front of him and hands it to me; I scan it with my eyes. It has all his contact info on it.

I stop my bitch routine for a second and take a good look at the man next to me. He's scary looking and big. His light eyes are kind, but there is damage lurking beneath their depths—as though he's been to war and back. For a strange reason, I trust him. This isn't another friend of Vincent's whom I should be afraid of.

I nod my head silently as my internal fume meter simmers down. The rest of the ride, I do nothing other than stare out the window, watching the magnificent red mountains ahead. I've never seen natural beauty like this in my entire life.

When we finally reach our destination, Slade pulls out my suitcases from the trunk and hands them to me. I thank him graciously.

Strutting into the lobby with my heels clicking against the floor, I take stock of what's around me. The hotel is beautiful and impossibly serene. The lobby is all tans, whites, and creams. Limestone floors and walls give the entire place an upscale but earthy feel. Glass windows encase the north side of the lobby, showing spectacular mountain views. It's simply perfect.

I check in with the concierge, a brunette, thank God, who accepts my firm's credit card along with my driver's license. Within seconds, my bags are taken and a cold towel is offered to me by a member of the hotel staff. I press it against my neck and forehead in relief as I'm told my room is ready.

Following the bellboy through an outdoor hallway, we stop to enter room 403. It's a stunning suite facing the desert land; tall sand-colored mountains loom in the distance. As he sets down my luggage, I step onto the terrace and see a small, round private fire pit and two chairs. The room is the epitome of seclusion and comfort. I wonder if this is the style Vincent is going toward for the Mile. From the work I've done so far, I know it isn't obvious and in-your-face bells and whistles like the Vegas Strip. Instead, it has all the gambling and excitement minus the phony factor. The files mentioned building the Milestone to blend with its surroundings, and I can't wait to see what he came up with.

I hand the bellboy a tip and he nods his thanks before exiting. Pulling off my shoes and shift dress and letting them drop onto the floor, I unceremoniously plop on the fluffy white bed to find a printed schedule on the pillow. Apparently, reservations for dinner have been made for me at six in the hotel lobby. Lauren must have taken care of this, thank goodness.

After showering, and put on a clean pair of jeans and a fresh shirt. After applying a minimal amount of makeup, I secure my dark hair with a clip. Grabbing a black cashmere sweater, I make my way to the hotel bar.

I try to relax in the black barstool, ordering a glass of white wine from the bartender. After my first sip, I decide that I can't let Vincent rule me. I have to separate my emotions from reality and just set out the facts. I pull out my phone and open my Notes app.

- **Since Vincent has returned...**

- I have a large new client and will likely make a lot
  more money
- He and I have agreed to leave the past where it belongs
- I still have my fantastic career and apartment

I want to write more, but I can't, because there IS nothing more. I shake out my shoulders, feeling satisfied. Just as Janelle and I discussed, there is literally zero to do other than get the work done; our history can't have any bearing on my career. Regardless of why we ended, we're finished. Today, I am Vincent's attorney, sent here to conduct due diligence on the Milestone. And Vincent is simply an important client.

Another sip of the wine and I smile confidently, feeling proud of my clear thought process and dissection of the issue when someone takes the seat next to mine.

"Hi. You're here."

I turn to the deep voice. The smile on his lips practically throws me off the seat. Fluttering takes over my stomach. I swallow hard, trying to regain a semblance of control.

"Y-yes, I-I guess I am. Here, I mean. I'm here."

Vincent's eyes crinkle at the corners, as if he's trying not to laugh at my stuttering.

"Come with me," he whispers with a smile. But I stay cemented in my seat, unmoving. A few moments pass and I watch as his initial happiness becomes tinged with apprehension.

More time is needed to sort this out—clearly, my list wasn't nearly expansive enough. This is Vincent Borignone, not a grocery list. The beat of my heart picks up its pace. "Actually," I start, clearing my throat. "I have a reservation soon. I shouldn't cancel."

We both turn our heads to peer inside the restaurant. My hope of delaying this meeting is smashed; the restaurant is completely empty. *Shit.*

"Dinner is with me tonight. Come." I can tell from his tone that he's annoyed with me. Standing up, he gives his large hand for me to take. I stare at it nervously, as though it may bite me.

He presses his lips in a firm line before exhaling. "We've got work to discuss, okay?"

"But, where are we—"

"For once in your life, don't think. Just come."

"Anytime a man tells me not to think—"

He cuts me off with deep laughter and I roll my eyes, trying to stop my smile. Does he remember the time at Goldbar when we had a similar conversation?

"We'll discuss work, yeah? I'm not trying to get you naked, Eve. There's no reason to be nervous." His dark eyebrows move up his forehead as if he's daring me.

I let out an awkward laugh. "Naked?" I swallow hard, the visual of a nude Vincent steamrolling through my head, down my body and settling in my core. "I don't think you're trying to get me... naked." I shake my head vehemently. "I mean, obviously not." A shiver runs up my arms as I force my eyes away from him.

"Exactly," he says, his voice deep and seductive. "We're doing business." He's so rational. I want to strangle him!

I internally huff, gathering myself. "Well, maybe I don't believe it's appropriate to do business in the evening hours." I want to sound haughty, but instead, my words come out like a nervous question.

His eyes narrow. *Oh, shit.*

Instead of cowering like the rest of the universe would likely do, I lift my head in defiance. The last thing I want is for Vincent to believe I'm anxious around him. I mean, if anyone should be awkward, it's him. I've done nothing wrong. If he's okay with seeing me, I'm more than okay to see him.

"Fine. If you think there is certain work better to do this evening, then I guess so be it." I hop off the stool, pretending that his hand isn't in my line of sight and that he isn't offering it to me. We get to the front of the hotel when I see a huge motorcycle sparkling under the orange lamplight; it's silver and chrome with a heavy black leather seat. I turn to Vincent with uncertainty, but he only smirks. We walk to the beast of a motorcycle and he lifts a small helmet from a bag hanging off to the side, securing it on my head before putting on his own. Jumping on, he gives me his hand. I remind myself: *Work purposes*. Holding onto his warm palm, I gingerly climb onto the back of the bike; our bodies are flush.

"Make sure you lean with me on the turns, okay? Don't be scared. There's no traffic. Driving on open roads is a dream."

I say a little thank you for this fully covered helmet because if he saw the look on my face, he'd know I'm dying inside. Between pressing against Vincent's hard back and the way my legs are splayed across this vibrating seat, the throb that started up in the restaurant is now pulsing.

I tentatively wrap my hands around his midsection, because hey —I don't want to die. Fortunately for my body, my hands immediately find the ripped muscles of his abdomen. God, he feels so good. It's almost like holding onto an unmovable wall. Moments later, we're off; the wind rushes around us like a curtain as the bike roars, my hair flying out from beneath the helmet.

"Oh, fuck it," I think, pressing my face against his muscled back and taking in his scent. *So good.*

11

VINCENT

I pull up to my trailer; it's on a quiet sandy patch on the rez. Getting off the bike first, I move to lift Eve in my arms, not wanting her legs to touch the hot pipes. I've burned myself before, and it sucks. Once she's steady on the ground, she pulls off her own helmet, shaking out her hair like some sexy shampoo commercial; except when she stops, it isn't perfect bouncy strands. Nope. It's a wild tangled mess. I smirk; her hair is exactly how I like it—natural and crazed.

"Shut it, Vincent." She giggles while trying to tame it down with her fingers.

"Let's go inside. I've got some meat marinating and ready to grill. You still like steak?"

She nods, her face tightening with anxiety. What Eve doesn't realize is I'm just as nervous as she; I'm just better at hiding it.

It doesn't take a genius to recognize that anytime Eve feels as though we're moving away from business, she freezes. I've got to slow the moment down for her. Keep us at a steady pace—for now. Every ounce of me wants to just *talk*. Get it all out there. But she's not ready to hear it.

"I've got a few files we should work through." I say the last part slowly, knowing that work will keep her comfortable around me.

"Yeah. Okay." She pushes back her thick hair, securing it with a clip. I give myself a mental pat on the back, glad to know that my plan for easing Eve is working.

I open the door, stepping directly into my living room. I turn, watching her eyes widen in surprise before turning back to me. Luckily, she isn't horrified. Actually, her face looks somewhat settled in relief.

Seven years ago, I shattered this woman and ruined her life. Everything she threw at me that night after the gala was deserved. No. I deserved worse. And now I'm back, and somehow, she's still here. I want to pull her in my arms and thank her. If she'd just give me a chance, I'd show her that I've given it all up. But I've got to make her believe that I'm true.

"Nice place," she tells me, a soft blush on her cheeks as her eyes zero in on my couch. Nothing is fancy, but it's all clean and comfortable.

I point to the left. "Kitchen." I turn, pointing to the opposite side of the trailer. "Bedroom and bathroom." I walk a few steps to the sink, seeing my two large marinated rib steaks have defrosted nicely. "How about I'll grill these out front and you make a salad?"

"Okay." Again, the hesitant nod.

My smile grows as I watch her straighten her back and walk toward the fridge with her head raised. Opening up my refrigerator as though it's her own, she pulls out some chopped red cabbage and washed spinach leaves, dropping them on the counter. She plunges her head back inside, probably noticing containers filled with grilled chicken and beef before coming back out again.

"Do you have mustard, olive oil, red wine vinegar?"

"Yeah." I pull out what she needs, my heart pounding—she remembers this is my favorite dressing. I open my small liquor cabinet, taking a bottle of red wine, two glasses, and an opener. Grabbing a handful of files we can review together, I finally step outside to fire up the grill.

While the meat cooks, I watch the mountains in the distance, taking a moment to thank God for my life. I never considered myself a God-fearing man, but between these vast mountains and the clear sky, it feels like denying the existence of a higher power is impossible. Compared to New York, where everything is man-made from the people to the buildings, it was easy to believe that I was in control of my own life and destiny. God's work is obscure in the big city. Out here though, is nothing but the truth. I look around and witness creation on a daily basis. I imagine Eve living with me here. Loving me. I picture her in my bed every morning and night.

I turn the steaks over, finding a perfect sear. A few minutes later, I pull them off the grill and onto the plate. Eve is sitting at the small picnic table to my right, watching me with a glazed look in her eyes as if she sees something more than just...me. The sun has set behind her, and she looks like an angel.

I take a seat, immediately moving to open the bottle. The last thing I want is to show my desperation for her, which would probably send her running into the mountains. I clear my throat. "I wanna take you hiking tomorrow around the area. See the land. Some cold beers and I'll pack lunch. Yeah?" I pour her a full glass, but only half for myself. I'm driving her back tonight and want to make sure my head is clear.

"I'm not so sure that's necessary."

"Well, it is," I reply firmly before clenching my fists to calm down. "It's important for you to know the surrounding area." She presses her lips together in contemplation.

Standing, she fills my plate with salad—taking care of me. I stare until she finally brings those big brown eyes to mine. *I miss you. I fuckin' love you, babe. Come back to me. Forgive me.* The words sit on the tip of my tongue, but I refuse to mess this up. I can't push her.

I clear my throat as she takes her seat. "I don't want you thinking I'm doing illegal shit here, anymore."

"I don't think that, Vincent." She shakes her head from side to side, her words sounding genuine.

"Well, you should know the score. If you're going to work for me, I

don't want you ever wondering if you'll be implicated in something."
I continue, giving her the details of how I set everything up in order
to safeguard the Mile from any possibility of seizure. She listens
quietly as I fill her in on details. I make sure to include the fact that
I'm no longer in the family and have cut myself out of all their dealings, legal and not. She listens intently, seemingly hanging onto
every word.

"Well, that's pretty crazy. I mean, I never thought you could—"

"Well, I have. Thank you for taking this chance on me. For
working with me on the Milestone. Seriously."

We stare at each other, an emotional and heavy silence between
us. Her brows furrow before she lifts the glass to her lips. Slicing up
her meat, she brings a piece of it to her lush mouth. I blink, knowing
that I'd do anything to have this woman's lips on mine. She catches
me staring, but I don't look away. *I can't.*

When we're finishing up, I pull out a set of architectural plans for
one of the spas. The designers submitted their ideas a few days ago,
and I've been reviewing them to decide the best option.

I move our plates to the end of the table before unrolling the large
sheets of paper, securing them with our glasses on opposite corners.
"I wanted to hear your opinion on this. There are two spa companies
that want to take over the space, but each of their lawyers put in
clauses that I'm not so sure about. They also have different visions for
the space."

"Retail leasing. One of my specialties." She smiles confidently,
moving to my side of the table so we're both looking at the plans from
the same view.

An hour passes and we're pouring over the minutia, keeping
focused as a team. Fuckin' heaven. I keep letting my arm brush
against hers and yet, she stays by my side.

When we finally leave to take her back to the hotel, I don't even
remember to clean up the table or bring the dishes in. All I see is her.

12

EVE

Vincent brings me back to my hotel, the perfect gentleman. I check my phone, seeing three missed calls from Janelle and one from Lauren. Nosy girls they are; obviously both want to know about the day. I take off all my clothes before walking into the beautiful bathroom to wash my face and brush my teeth. The cold marble feels amazing against my feet, hot from riding.

The next morning, I wake up with my cell next to my head—I forgot to call anyone back. Picking up the room phone and dialing in-room dining, I order a hot coffee and an egg-white vegetable omelet.

I take my time in the shower before finding a plush bathrobe hanging behind the door. I try it on, reveling in its softness. Dropping in the terrace chair, I let myself daydream about Vincent's life out here on the rez—simple, yet straightforward. No frills, yet incredibly satisfying.

No one has ever taken care of me in the way Vincent has. Behind the size, the strength, and the tough façade, he gives me this... warmth. I've been stressing so much about him lately, and I just want to relax. He isn't pressuring me, and I have no reason to feel nervous.

My doorbell rings, and I pad over to the door barefoot. I open it, expecting breakfast.

"Rise 'n shine." His black hair is windblown, and his skin a perfectly dark tan. My throat dries. "Gotta get going early before sun gets too hot," he tells me with a smile.

"You could have called." I'm annoyed. Tightening my robe around my waist, shyness comes over me. Vincent, on the other hand, doesn't seem fazed in the slightest.

"Nice room," he states casually, welcoming himself inside. Taking a seat on the white couch in front of the bed, he leans back cool and calm as though he's the one staying here.

"I'll wait. Get dressed," he states succinctly. I roll my eyes before taking a good look at the man before me. Scanning him, my feet suddenly grow heavy, keeping me rooted to the spot. Every single thing in this room from the slept-in white sheets to the beautiful terrace to the gorgeous floors fade away—everything except him.

The old Vincent would give me a smirk, telling me with a cocky expression that he's reading me like an open book. Instead, what I see in his face shows something closer to yearning.

I clear my throat and turn around, entering the small changing area that's connected to the bathroom. I change into a pair of Lululemon black leggings, a fitted sports bra that gives me great cleavage, and matching spandex tank top. Finishing off the outfit with a pair of sneakers and my hair in a high ponytail, I check myself out in the bathroom mirror.

Feeling confident, I step back into the bedroom, noticing my room service already arrived.

Vincent looks me up and down. "Sorry babe. As good as you look in those pants, you're gonna need jeans to ride." He shrugs a huge shoulder as a sexy half smile forms on his lips.

I groan, turning back into the bathroom to change, albeit grudgingly. Truthfully, I loved riding on his bike. I'm itching to get back on, but he doesn't need to know that. I come back into the room, updated. "Better?" I ask, my voice syrupy sweet.

He stares at me mutely as his eyes rove up and down my body. "I want to take you to the Mile," he starts, his voice rough. "After, we'll hike the valley of Fire State Park."

Sitting up and turning his eyes away from me, he pours two cups of steaming coffee from the large silver carafe, finishing mine with cream and sugar.

"Where's the park?" I ask as he hands me a mug. Putting my nose to the coffee, I smell the sweet and nutty aroma. With just a whiff, I feel refreshed.

"It's a nature preserve about sixteen miles south of Overton. I'd show you a photo, but it's better if you're surprised."

"Are there snakes?" I ask nervously. "I'm not down with snakes."

"Nah," he shakes his head. "I mean, they exist. But chances are slim we'll see any."

"Slim, like, slim to none? Or slim, like, there's a possibility greater than two percent?"

He lets out a deep chuckle that I feel straight down in my belly. "Chill, city girl. I'll be with you the whole time. Nothing to be afraid of when I'm with you, yeah?" His words come out slow and thick, feeling and sounding like truth.

"Okay." Lifting the coffee to my mouth, I watch as his gaze moves to where my lips press against the cup's rim. It dawns on me that this man—New York City mobster, has morphed into an outdoorsy biker. I try not to smile at the irony.

"What are you thinking about?" He leans closer to me.

"Wouldn't you like to know," I sass.

"No, actually." He shakes his head in mock seriousness and I slap his arm, laughing.

Sitting down beside him on the couch with nothing but a sliver of space between us, I lift my fork and knife to enjoy my omelet. He's scanning headlines on his phone while I eat and read my own work emails. Our quiet is filled with comfort. Everything about this moment feels natural.

* * *

We get off his bike and I immediately take out my phone to see if I have any missed calls.

"I forgot how obsessed you are with being on time. Do me a favor and give me your phone." He puts out his hand.

"No way," I exclaim, looking up into his face, warmed and slightly sweaty from the helmet.

"Come on. What are you afraid of? Missing a call from work? If anyone complains, just say the phone service was shit." His eyes are mischief.

I bite my lip, considering his dare. I haven't taken a vacation for myself in years, choosing instead to spend any days off just lounging in my apartment and reading. What would happen if I actually listened to Vincent right now? Normally, I am diligent in following all timelines and schedules. Every billable minute counts. Truthfully, I'm tired of it.

I do the unthinkable, handing him the phone.

"Ah!" he shouts. "The girl listens." His voice is triumphant. I roll my eyes as he opens a bottle of water and hands it to me.

I look around. "My God, Vincent. This is..." I'm at a loss for words. I simply cannot believe the beauty of what's in front of me. Other than the size, the style is similar to the Freedom Towers in New York City. Four low buildings nestle into the mountains. With glass and steel façades, they act as mirrors, picking up the oranges, reds, silvers, and golds of the mountains. They're incredibly modern, but because of the play of light, look seamlessly woven into the Nevada desert. Simply unbelievable.

He clears his throat and I stare back up at his strong and serious demeanor. "You like it?"

I nod my head.

"It occupies roughly one mile of land, hence the name Milestone..." He continues, and I listen, completely enraptured. The boy I knew has evolved into a captivating and mature man.

He brings me to each of the buildings, showing me what's completed. Everything is both modern and five-star, but the complex stays true to the mountains and the desert; it's unlike anything I've ever seen. Vincent has really done it. He's astounding. After the tour, we jump back on his bike and head toward the State Park.

We arrive, and Vincent steps off his bike first before helping me down. It occurs to me that he doesn't need to carry me, but I can't seem to tell him no. Once he sets me onto the ground, he pulls out some food from his saddlebag. I walk by his side until we reach the park.

He points forward and I look up. "Red sandstone. Amazing, right?"

In front of me are red-and-silver-swirl mountains. He takes my hand gently, bringing me over to a shaded picnic table and sets out our lunch, making sure I'm sitting with the best view.

We eat and joke around, my mood lightening. All of our past is on the backburner as we get to know the updated versions of ourselves.

He tells me more about Slade, who he says is like a brother to him. It turns out that Slade had a rough stint after spending over six years in special operations.

"He seems really decent," I tell him in all seriousness.

"Yeah. The more you get to know him, the better he gets."

I raise my eyebrows and purse my lips, a facial combination that's got New York City Blue Houses written all over it. "Don't tell me you've got a bromance."

Vincent laughs. "Well, he's a good-looking guy. Can you blame me?" We both laugh as he squints his eyes in that cocky New York way and here we are again, just two city kids playing around.

He gives me a wicked grin. "It's getting hot, right?"

Before I can answer, he pours a bottle of water all over my head. I take a sharp inhale before screaming, and he just laughs.

"You're gonna pay for that," I exclaim. My hair is going to frizz like crazy now that it's been doused with water. I didn't even bring my hot tools with me, figuring that dry shampoo would secure me for the week. *Shit!*

I get up, pouring my own water over his head and feeling highly vindicated. The water drips off the tips of his black hair, hitting his sharp cheekbones. He stares up me hotly. *Holy shit.* Vincent is so sexy it's insane.

"You still like looking, huh?"

His comment makes me angry and I give him the stink eye, which makes him laugh louder.

We spend the rest of the day hiking. Each time he helps me up a tall rock, my heart patters. His hand is just so massive and swallows my tiny one so easily. My body loves it.

Over a few hours, we get to really talking. Vincent tells me about his life in prison and how the Mile came to be; he talks about his unlikely friendship with the warden and how much that support meant to him. I know there's more he isn't telling me, but still, he's opening up more than I would have imagined.

We find a nice large, high, and flat rock to take a break. Sitting down together, our legs dangle off the side as we stare out at the setting sun.

I want to talk to him, too. Something inside me aches to connect; it's been so long since I've had that with anyone. "You know," I say nervously. "I worked so hard to be in this position at work—" I pause, giving my attention to a group of three making their way up the mountain, packs on their backs. I let myself take another second or two, needing to sort through my thoughts before continuing. Vincent sits quietly, giving me time.

"I should feel fulfilled, right?" I question. "Instead, though, I just feel exhausted and totally...burned out." I put my finger on the rock, moving some dirt around.

"After my first large paycheck, I bought myself this beautiful silver desk clock from Tiffany's. Actually, I bought myself a lot of stuff. And now, when I see them, I want to burn it all. I thought those things would make me happy, but they don't. It's like..." I lift my head and hands in aggravation. "Whenever I hit a milestone, I find myself looking to the next thing, because the satisfaction I was supposed to have never comes. When can I just stop and be happy where I am? I thought once I had the material things, I'd feel like I arrived or something. I worked for this. I bled for this. But it's not...enough."

He turns his head, sadness coating his eyes. I wait for him to speak, but instead he stays silent, urging me with his eyes to continue.

"Still," I say. "I love the independence the job brings. I love the fact that the money I make is all my own. I'm sorry to say this, but I just love making money. Sometimes I check my bank account and I'm like, so relieved. And thrilled. And I worked my ass off to get it, too. After being poor all my life..." I pause a second before continuing. "I also helped Janelle with the down payment on her salon, and...I think I'll make partner one day..." my voice trails off.

Vincent moves his arm, brushing it against mine. He leans so close, I can smell his scent: dark and woodsy. He's almost close enough to kiss. I wonder if the dark scruff on his jaw is rough or soft. I drop my hands on the rock, keeping myself from reaching up and touching him.

"I understand your need to feel financially secure," he says softly. "But there are other things you could do that would give you all of those benefits as well. Something you love that would also give you satisfaction. You've worked hard and I get it's difficult to step back after clawing your way to the top. You thought this is what you wanted, but it isn't what you thought it would be. Why should you have to make yourself suffer? Fuck it. You've got one life, and you are allowed to change your mind, Eve. Money can be made in many ways —trust me."

"But, what would I even do?" I ask questioningly, eyes fixated on his face. Yes, he's gorgeous. But in this moment, all I see is the man inside.

"Well, you're part of the Kids Learning Club, right?" A small smile plays on his lips.

I blink, the new wing coming into the forefront of my mind. Like the sun in front of me, the truth sets. "Vincent? Have you donated anything recently?" I stare into his eyes, wondering if it's possible he would do such a thing. What I see shining back at me is a definite yes.

"Sure," he shrugs casually. "I may have donated something for someone I've been missing."

I stare up into his handsome face, speechless. I open my mouth to speak when he lifts his hand up.

"No. Don't give me that. It means something to you and the truth is, it means something to me, too. Those kids deserve a chance. I believe in the Club's mission, okay?"

I nod my head, wanting to believe him. He admitted before that he kept tabs on me—which still infuriates me to no end. Still, I'm glad that at least the Kids Learning Club benefited from it.

He stands, wiping the back of his jeans with his palms before taking my hand to help me up. It's getting dark as we shuffle down the trail. Vincent supports me as we walk; it's trickier on the way down than it was on the way up. Finally, we make it back to his bike. After handing me my phone and watch, his phone rings. Lowering his head, he checks the caller ID. Instead of answering, he clicks IGNORE. The ringing stops, and I immediately go on alert.

"Who was that?" I ask probingly.

He turns as though ready to speak. But, he doesn't.

"Well?" I ask again, a little annoyed.

"It was Tom."

"Oh?" My hands move to my hips as my emotions start gearing up for level-ten-magnitude anger.

"I'm out of the family, Eve. He's still my boy, though," he says with a decided finality.

I let my eyes move up and down his body. "Are you packing right now?"

He stares at me, amused, before bringing his hands down and lifting his dark shirt. There's only gorgeous tan skin and mouth-watering muscles; no guns in sight. My gaze moves down his jeans next, stopping at his ankles. I look back up at him pointedly. "Lift your jeans, Borignone."

He laughs out loud, the sound lighting something up in my chest that I thought was dead.

"You used to help me, remember?" he winks. *Oh God, do I.* Bending down, he brings up the bottom of his pants to show me his ankles, proving to me he no longer carries weapons.

I try not to show it, but my heart wildly pounds inside my chest. I want to stop it, but I can't.

13

VINCENT

We stop at her hotel. I get off the bike first to lift her off, taking an extra few moments to hold her before setting her down. Staring into her eyes, I want to kiss the hell out of her. But the look I see in return is still tinged with some anxiety. I swallow, knowing the key to Eve is still patience.

She saunters away without a backward glance and I'm left staring mutely at her perfect ass. She enters the hotel lobby and my phone rings again. I check the caller ID. It's Tom again.

"Yo."

"Vincent. How many fucking times do I have to call you? Look man," he sighs. "Things are getting hot here, and you're not answering your goddamn phone."

"I've told you too many goddamn times. I'm not part of that shit anymore."

"It's your father. He's getting angrier. Darker. Doing shit you wouldn't imagine. And he's still fuming over your leaving—"

"Look, I've got some work to do. I'll talk to you—"

"Don't you fuckin' hang up the phone!" he barks. "Your father is a dangerous man, or have you forgotten? I can feel bad shit coming your way. You know I've got a sense for these things. He blames you, Vincent."

"Me? What the fuck did I do? I'm not the one who aligned with lunatics. I'm not the one who got into business with untrustworthy men."

"You left—that's what you did. And I can feel it in my bones. He's comin' for you."

"No," I growl back. "I'm all the way out here. I've got Slade by my side nearly every damn moment. When the Mile opens, money will pour in and he'll calm down."

"Open up your eyes, brother." I can hear the stress in his voice over the line. "Because you aren't in the fold, you don't know the shit that's heating up. You've gotta trust me on this," he says desperately. "Your father has changed. You said it in lockup, but I didn't really see it until now. He's got a serious screw loose."

"I know who my father is. But I can't care anymore. I just can't."

"And Eve? You still tryin' to get her back?"

"Yup." My voice leaves no room for negotiation.

"All right, man. What can I say?" he says dejectedly. "Just do me a favor and watch yourself. Don't let your guard down."

I hang up and head directly back to the Mile. There's a large art installation coming tomorrow and I want to make sure the space is ready.

14

VINCENT

One Year Ago

"Vincent," the warden calls my name, shaking me out of my work-induced trance. When I'm focusing like this on the Mile, I'm on another mental plane. I don't need to eat, drink, or take a piss for hours on end when I'm in this zone. I look out the barred window, noticing what looks like a torrential downpour.

I turn my head to face him, straightening my back. "What's up?"

"Dinner's on. I didn't want to interrupt you, but you know how the inmates talk when they don't see you at meals."

"Yeah, I know." I stand, cracking my neck. Tension is always higher when people are stuck inside all day.

No one knows the warden and I are friends, not even my boys. Hell would land on me if word ever got out. But I'm thankful for the guy. Our weekly chess sessions where we talk about current events helps to keep my mind sane. Otherwise, I'd probably rot in here, like so many men do.

Our friendship started simply. He'd been reading my emails about the Mile, as prescribed by the judge, and started to ask some questions. Before I *knew it, he became a great source of information. His brother is a builder and father an architect, so he knows a thing or two. And while the family negotiated the computers and email access for me with the DA before my entry, it's my friendship with the warden that actually gives me the time and space I need to build the Milestone.*

We shake hands before he cuffs me, passing me off to a guard who brings me down the steps to the chow hall. My crew bangs on the table as I enter, a show of respect. The men around us quiet for a moment, looking down in a combination of terror and worship. Between fucking up Crow and creating the Mile, I've developed a reputation of power. I may be in handcuffs, but I'm the one leading the guard to the table and everyone here knows it.

"Fuckin' stop that shit," I grumble, annoyed. The banging immediately stops. I turn my head around the room, feeling a change in the air. Everyone seems twitchy.

I turn to Tom, who's laughing at something Chris is telling him. "What are we eating tonight? Ribs?" I stare at the gruel in their plates. The guard removes the cuffs from my wrists before stepping away.

"Sorry Vincent," Tom replies. "Tonight, we've got Veal Milanese with a side of fried garlic and artichokes. Elios delivered your favorite a few minutes ago. Even brought a nice chunk of Parmigiana with fresh crusty bread and butter."

I chuckle. Elios is our favorite Italian on the Upper East Side of New York City, and Tom and I have been dreaming of it for years now.

I walk over to the line still filled with people waiting for grub. The first guy notices me and immediately steps back so I can cut. There is a pecking order here, and things move smoothly because of it. My eyes scan the shitty food options when—seemingly out of nowhere—a fist comes barreling into my cheek before a weapon is plunged into my thigh. I'm caught off guard, momentarily stunned.

"Fuck you!" the guy screams. I throw an arm around his neck and turn his back to my front, incapacitating him while gaining my bearings. The entire place is silent, watching in shocked confusion as a little pissant tries to fight me.

Seeing as he's black and this entire place is divided by color and race, the white inmates start to mumble, likely taking his act as a personal attack. He's struggling, but I keep him in my hold, waiting for a guard to break this up and take him away. The last thing I want to do is spend a few weeks in the hole for fighting back.

The talk in the room turns louder. The yelling begins.

One.

Two.

Three.

That's all it takes for the entire chow hall to turn on each other. I can hear the walkie-talkies going off around me as an alarm bell turns on. It's deafening.

Meanwhile, this guy—who I've never even seen before—keeps trying to get out of my grip. He moves his head around, trying to bite me.

"My f-f-fam," he attempts to speak, but I shut his mouth with my hand, holding him against my chest. Moving my head to the side, I take a good look at his tear-stained face. He's nothing but a kid, barely looks eighteen. And fuck, but he's crying. I'm restraining him, but not causing pain.

The chaos continues around us when I realize he's trying to actually tell me something.

"What is it?" I ask tightly, lifting my hand as blood soaks through my pants. I'm still keeping him in my clutches, but letting him tell his message to me.

"Fuck the Borignone mafia!" he says, saliva dripping from his mouth onto my palm. His forehead is in my grip and I'm holding his head tightly. One twist and I could break his neck. I pull his head tighter, letting him know if he tries anything, his life is done.

He takes heavy pants through his nose. "Killed my whole family. Burned my whole house down with them in it. Just because I was short. I hope you all die and rot in hell!"

Before I can process what he just said, tear gas is thrown into the hall, and we all go down.

* * *

I'm waiting in the cafeteria for my father's bi-monthly visit. I got a corner table by a window. Prime real estate.

The family's business has been deteriorating in the last few years and it's obvious to me that as of late, it's only gotten worse. The men in here with me are organized and follow the proper command. But from what I've been gathering, disorganization is starting to reign back in New York. Worse, the family has been inducting sloppy kids with no sense of decency or respect. Rumors have circulated about the Boss Brotherhood MC getting in touch with my father on the outside and have struck some sort of deal. It's hard to believe, considering the fact that here on the inside, we're enemies. I'd never imagined the family would work with a bunch of skinheads, but my sources don't lie.

My father comes across from me, sitting down in the blue plastic chair and pulling it closer to the table. "Vincent," he says calmly, "I want to know if—"

"Not today," I say, effectively cutting him off. He squints his eyes in confusion. Clenching and unclenching my fists, I know I'm going to need to keep calm in order to have this talk.

He leans back into his chair, casually draping one leg over the other as though he were sitting at the opera as opposed to a prison.

"I wanna know why I keep hearing about our nephews getting more...excited around town." I say the word 'excited' slowly, so he understands I mean more aggressive. "Nephews" has always been our code word for younger men in the family. "Word is, they're losing control. Control is paramount, yeah?"

"I guess you can say the new nephews are more excitable. Especially these days," he replies casually. "With the changing times, this is the path the family is taking."

I sit back in my chair, crossing my arms over my chest. "You have to get rid of them. They're nothing but tr—"

"Well Vincent, if you want to keep growing your family, new children are a must."

My heart pounds as I turn my head away from my father and toward the sea of convicts. This fuckin' life.

"I don't like this route," I practically spit the words out. "You know I'd *never okay this. I hear some of them have priors." I move myself closer to him and lower my voice. "Sexual assault? Stalking? Petty theft? What the fuck is that about? It's unacceptable," I say quietly with gritted teeth.*

"Too bad you're not home and don't get a vote." He puts a hand in his jacket pocket, casually pulling out a piece of spearmint gum.

I shake my head disbelievingly.

He looks me over. "It takes numbers to maintain a stronghold. Otherwise, new kids come from other places and try to take what's ours."

"But that was never our way," I say tightly. "We're better than that. Than them." I point my finger to the men around us.

"It's where we are," he states succinctly, chewing his gum and watching me pointedly, daring me to disagree.

"You know the guys I grew up with and always fucking despised?" I draw a large B with my finger on the table. He sits up, nodding in understanding that I'm talking about the Boss Brotherhood. He knows our beef with them here in prison is dark. "Inviting them for a birthday party is the biggest mistake yet. I won't attend if they're included."

He leans forward, clearly aggravated. "You better fuckin' be there, Vincent. Birthday parties are. Not. Negotiable." His voice is a threatening growl.

"I'm not sanctioning this." I seethe, trying to keep my voice low despite my pounding pulse. "Neo-Nazis? These guys are dirty. You want to contaminate our lives with parasites?" I question. My body grows hot.

"What you fail to realize is while you've been gone, the landscape has changed. We've got to make sure these new kids on the block don't take our candy."

I move closer to him, our heads practically glued together over the table.

"These new nephews of ours are nothing but trouble," I say, keeping my voice measured. "They'll never be effective members, and they'll only bring us down in the end." My mind rails. "Who the fuck is even in control of bringing in these morons? Good men are hard to find and even harder to train. The muscle we hired to help us out for the Mile were ex-Israeli Defense Force men. I spent months scouting them out and interviewing to make sure they were legitimate. These choices you're making are fucked. Ya hear me?"

Shock and anger mar his face; my father was always a narcissist, but his ego has grown tremendously in the last few years. I can tell I'm pushing him right now, but he's gotta hear it.

The bell rings, letting us know our time is up.

"Listen to me," I tell him as I stand, pushing my chair back aggressively and pointing my finger in his face, "show a little integrity—"

"No, son. You listen to me." He stands up quickly, grabbing me by the collar despite the no-contact rule. I can see a vein popping in the center of his forehead. "This is my goddamn show. My fucking party. Who's invited? I say who's invited! You're nothing without me. I'm the leader. You don't take a fuckin' piss without my okay," he exclaims.

A guard pulls us apart, cold cuffs linking my hands behind my back as I'm roughly escorted away. I look around quickly. Luckily, with everyone hugging their loved ones, our altercation has seemingly gone unnoticed by the other inmates.

I get back to my cell, sitting down on my cot as I'm locked back inside the cage. The bars close with a clang. Lifting my head to the small window, I stare up at the blue sky—free and clear of clouds. Somehow, in what feels like the first time in my life, I see things for what they are. I've had flashes of this truth, but now, it's here.

What the hell am I doing in here? Paying a debt and taking the fall.

Why did I leave the love of my life, stage an ending, effectively ruining Eve's world? To keep her safe from the life I live.

I grip the side of my bed. I've got to get out of the family, or sooner or later, I'll be back behind bars or dead.

Ever since I came to prison, things on the outside with the family have disintegrated. The new guys they're bringing into the fold? Sloppy. Hiring the BB to run guns for us? Disgusting. Over my dead body would I ever align with those fucks.

I used to believe leaving the East Coast and beginning gaming would allow me to stay as part of the family without dealing with its day-to-day business. I figured my physical departure would be enough. I was wrong. The only way to be free is to leave the fold completely.

I've told myself, all my life, that love and loyalty are who we are. Borignone mafia is power and strength. Borignone mafia is allegiance. I never considered us on the same level as these dirty street gangs. But now, it's obvious the only family glue is greed. My father doesn't care what he does, so long as the family stays on top. If that means selling us out, he's willing. I'm not sure if Antonio Borignone was always this way, or if he's changed. But regardless, this is where we stand—on opposite sides of the bay. I'd never imagined myself totally breaking free from the family; the stakes alone could mean my life. But for true freedom? It's worth the risk.

I drop my head in my hands. I've got to think strategically. If the family is doing business with that scum, it's ten times more likely our work on the outside has turned into disorder. Luckily, the Milestone is set up and so tightly organized, it can't be affected by any of their illegal business endeavors. My chest loosens. I'm glad to know the Mile's secure.

Ideas come and go into my head until I finally see a light go off. I've got to continue making myself invaluable. So much so, they can't kill me without risking their own business. My father prizes money above all things, and he'll do whatever he has to—so long as I line his pockets.

I'll leave the family and turn myself into their business partner instead. I won't have to take any fall of theirs as my own. I will give them that option as the only one. Otherwise, I'll take death. But if they choose to kill me, they'll be losing out on all the money. I'd bet my father will take what I offer.

Another thought jumps front and center: I need to call my lawyer and have him remove me from every single deed and business owned by the family. My ties must be totally severed. I raise my arms, grabbing the bottom of my shirt and pulling it up and off my head to stare at the tattoo on my arm. I'm sure I can find a way to blend it into something else. Get a nice sleeve when I'm out—cover this shit up and at least make the insignia less noticeable. I see Eve's name blended into the swirls and feel an immediate sense of calm.

Eve. Jesus, I miss her. I shut my eyes, ignoring the fact that I'm in a cold dark cell and picture her face. If I focus hard enough, I can even smell the coconut scent of her shampoo. What would she say if she knew I left the family? I imagine her smile when she hears the news. She wraps her arms around my neck, squealing with delight. I keep my eyes screwed shut, smiling at the images moving through my mind's eye.

15

VINCENT

"Vincent," she says, opening the door to her room. Her voice is smooth and sweet in the way I love. There is no doubt that my name was meant to be on those lips.

I bend down, kissing her soft cheek and taking in her clean scent. Her body shudders. "Hey." She smells absolutely perfect. Like fresh soap and coconut cream.

"Come in," she turns and I follow her inside. "So, what are we doing for today? I know Kimber mentioned plans to look through files at your office?" She moves around quickly, not making eye contact as she grabs her tablet off the desk along with her phone and e-reader, dropping them into a black bag.

Instead of replying right away, I just stand there, staring. How many years did I spend imagining her just like this, doing something mundane? My fantasies were never overly done. It's Eve in her normal habits: freshly showered. Sweaty after our workout at the gym. Cooking in my kitchen. Reading in bed next to each other while she compulsively highlights passages in a textbook, wearing my shirt. We don't have much time before she heads back to California. The clock on our week is ticking, and I've got to solidify us before she goes.

She smiles innocently as I clear my throat. "We'll go to my office first."

"Okay cool. Are we gonna ride there?" Her voice is hopeful.

"Hell yeah," I grin, noticing she's already wearing her jeans.

Instead of walking out, we both hesitate by the door. The air between us changes. I stare at her full lips and round brown eyes. I need her mouth on mine. I grip the keys in the palm of my hand, attempting to maintain control.

Throat moving in a hard swallow, I can tell she wants this, too. Instinct says to throw her on the bed. Rip her clothes off. Make her come so hard until she's yelling my name. But what if she refuses and everything comes crashing down? There's still so much to talk about.

"Take her," my blood roars, dick hardening in my jeans.

Licking her lips, her eyes scan me from head to toe. Her face is flushing, eyes dilating and body begging. She needs me. I can feel it.

I need to gather myself. I clench my fists, the keys digging into my palm. *Not now*, my mind pounds.

She brings her bag to her hip and I turn to the door, holding it open for her to walk through. After a long pause, she does.

16

EVE

Vincent's office isn't fancy. In fact, it's just another trailer on the rez. When we walk in, Slade's stepping out, talking on the phone. I hear him mention something about camera equipment. He raises his palm to us in "hello" before getting on his bike and driving away.

Vincent steps behind me. He's so near, I can feel his body heat; I'm warming from the inside. Today, things are different between us. The tension is becoming impossible to bear. I know there are still so many issues. But overarching everything is my need for him. I want to feel that closeness again. I can't believe how long I've gone without it —without *him*.

He points to the left. "Kimber works out of here with us, but she's on-site today. Slade takes this front area, and I use the back. Files and everything you need are where I am."

I scan the room, realizing the screens and computers they're all using are seriously high-tech. As relaxed as Vincent is, I'm reminded that he's running a multi-million-dollar industry.

We walk together into his office, closed off by a door from where Slade and Kimber work. The entire room is filled with bookshelves, and they're packed to the brim. I have zero doubt Vincent has read everything in here. Against the window are silver file cabinets, which I assume are what I'll be going through. There's also a large desk outfitted with two large monitors, and a brown leather couch off to the side.

"When did you get all these books?" My fingers lightly graze their spines as I read their titles, one by one.

"I kept notes of what I read in prison. And whatever I loved, I ordered for myself when I got out here."

I want to ask where he wants me to begin when my bag falls off my shoulder, clattering onto the floor. I drop down to my knees, meaning to pick it up. But when I raise my head, what I see freezes me to the ground. Vincent stands tall above me, tatted up and rough. The look on his face has me so turned on, I'm afraid to blink. The slightly reserved man from the last few weeks has been uncovered and in his place is the real Vincent—raw and intense. My gaze moves to his thick-corded neck, tan from riding, and down to his jeans where I come face to face with his enormous erection, punching through his jeans.

"Vincent?" My voice shakes with nerves. *God*, but he is just colossal, making this small room look more like a dollhouse than a small office. I want him so badly my brain literally clouds over with lust.

"Yeah, baby." His voice is deep as he extends a hand to me. On shaky legs, I rise. There are conversations to be had. But right now, I can see and feel nothing but us.

The last seven years, I gravitated toward men I could control. Clearly, that isn't going to happen here. But—I want to try. What would Vincent do, if for once, I was the one in charge?

"Wait," the word leaves my lips and he pauses—for just a second. His eyes assess the situation as my body trembles from his proximity. He takes another step, closer still. Could it be as good as it was back in college? So much time has passed; I'm not even sure what was real and what was simply my imagination.

He lifts me into his arms effortlessly, placing me on the leather couch, so I'm sitting, facing him. Dropping to his knees before me, he takes my head in his hands. Pushing back my hair so all he can see is my face, his dark eyes bore into mine.

"Say yes," he asks. His voice is gravel, almost desperate. "I'd never touch you unless you wanted it."

I blink once, twice, and slowly move my head up and down. My body has taken over.

He inches closer until his mouth is pressed against mine. I can feel a small sliver of tongue slide between my lips. "Oh, God," I moan, shifting my body horizontal and pulling him onto me. He rubs his mouth over mine gently and whisper-soft. Not entering. Not going fast like I wish he would.

I'm shaking. He's barely moved and my panties are drenched. He continues to do nothing other than tease. My legs open wider in anticipation, but he's taking his damn time.

He licks at my ear, sucking down the column of my neck. I think I'm begging him to undress me, but I can't be sure. *Is he really here?* I shut my eyes and inhale, everything feels right. I know—it's Vincent. Mine.

I shift my body, trying to align us. Moving my hands down to unbutton my pants, I'm yearning to get naked. I need skin on skin. He moves his fingers to where mine are, unfastening my jeans for me before pulling them off. Lifting me up with a muscled arm, my shirt and bra fly off next. We're fused, breathing each other in until our inhales are completely synchronized. I grip his back beneath his shirt and lightly score my nails against his skin. He hisses and I smile at the power I feel.

I'm desperately waiting for him to get naked. I pull at the waist of his jeans and luckily, he takes the hint. His leather jacket comes off first, followed by his black Henley. The air in the room leaves as I take the biggest inhale of my life. I thought I knew the body beneath the shirt, but apparently, my imagination didn't do him justice. Vincent is absolutely ripped. The leanness of his youth has been replaced with heavy muscle and swirls of black, riotous tattoos. I notice a long scar on his lower abs, but there's no time to examine. I need his hands on me. My mouth dries as I watch his pants fall to the ground. His underwear is next. Vincent's dick is a sight to behold—perfect. Mouthwateringly thick and long. His body is a work of art.

He moves to the edge of the couch, nostrils flaring in desire. My heart pounds. I'm naked and for the first time in seven years, completely vulnerable and at a man's mercy. Control? Gone. Nothing could ever prepare me for this. His dark gaze roams every inch of my body and I subconsciously arch my back, thrusting my full breasts toward him. I yearn for him to see me in the way only Vincent ever has.

"Your body. You're so beautiful, baby. Your nose. Your lips. That mouth. Everything about you..." He moves his large palm down from my stomach all the way to my toes and back up again. "I'm insane for you. Stupid for you. God, Eve, everything about you calls to me. We need to talk, but I can't stop right now."

Talk? I can barely breath.

He lowers his mouth to my nipple and my entire body convulses with his first suck. I'm turning mindless as he shifts, lining himself up with me and sliding his dick up and down, agonizingly slow, my wetness coating us both and driving me insane. I clutch at his neck, wrapping my legs around his waist and raising my body higher, angling myself to catch him. But I can't. Why won't he just get inside me already?

"Vincent!" I yell.

I can feel his smirk against my shoulder. "I fuckin' missed you." Back and forth, he drags his heavy cock over that bundle of nerves, wreaking havoc on my insides. My body pounds with desire and need.

"Missed the way you smell. Your soft body in my hands." His voice rumbles at my ear as he gently pulls my hair, moving my head back before dropping his head to take another deep suck of my nipple. My pussy clenches. "You're my life," he growls. "My every- thing. Do you know that?" His damp breaths move to my ear. "I've been dreaming of you nonstop. In every move I make. It's always you. Only you. Since you, there was no one else. Do you hear me?"

This man owns me.

I want to speak, to tell him everything, but I can only whimper. Every ounce of blood has left my brain.

His eyes, now coal black, lock on mine. "I need to know you hear me. That you want this. Tell me again," he insists.

I shiver, realizing he isn't going to continue until I give him full consent. I grab the back of his head in an attempt to force his lips back to mine, but he won't move.

"For fuck's sake, Vincent. Now!" I beg.

He chuckles. "Just what I need to hear." He fills me entirely, all at once, and my insides pulse against him. It's so good, it's shocking. His fingers move down to my clit and I throw my head back, moaning loudly. My body wants to bind itself to his. Seal us together.

"Good girl," he whispers as I tighten my legs around him. "Need to hear you. Need to hear those moans, understand? Been waiting seven years for this. For you."

He drives into me hard and deep only to pull back in a slow drag as if he were savoring me. Pleasure like hot lava pools in my core, a feeling I haven't felt since Vincent himself all those years ago. No, it couldn't have been this good.

"...Don't stop," I groan as he mumbles a soft curse, pushing deeper.

Beads of sweat drip from his body and onto my breasts. I stare up at him, wanting to memorize his face—just like this. I can scarcely believe I'm on my back with Vincent above me.

"I have to taste you," he mumbles, voice heavy.

Sliding out of me, he moves off the couch and drops to his knees. I can feel his hands, hot against my skin spread my thighs apart. The warmth of his lips and wet tongue fall directly on my center and with a firm and hot lick, my lower body clamps like a vise, ankles locking around his head. My entire world shimmers while he continues to drink me in.

In a sex-drunken daze, I'm brought onto his lap on the floor. I wrap my arms around him tightly as he begins to fuck me in earnest with too many years' worth of tension. Bending his body, he captures my mouth in a deep kiss. It's desperate, our tongues swirling together.

I can taste a trace of myself on him. Our hands clasp, fingers lacing together. Clinging to his huge body, I take everything he gives.

He pants as his movements deepen. Rolling his hips, a heavy hand cups the underside of my breasts as his angle shifts. He's hitting *that* spot. Like a cyclone, another wave of pleasure moves through me. My world explodes as he roars, collapsing on top of me with his own release. We're a bundle of sweat and pounding hearts.

"Thank God," I say out loud, tears rolling down my face as I press my cheek against his shoulder. *This.* We have so much to talk about, but I feel the truth now. My heart always knew it.

Vincent wraps me up tightly in his arms, pressing a hot kiss against my lips. "Fuckin' love you. Always will."

After we somewhat stabilize, we stand. Vincent presses his lips on every inch of my body before covering me with my clothing. *This man.*

"Let's stop. Get you some stuff you'll need at my place."

"Why not the hotel?" My voice comes out as a rasp.

"Takes too long. Need you in my bed," he grumbles, voice low and deep.

"My clothes?"

"Not necessary."

We get back onto his bike and ride to the nearest pharmacy. Vincent struts up and down the aisles, picking up a toothbrush, shampoo and conditioner, and face and body wash with quick efficiency. I'm laughing as I practically chase him down, trying to keep up with his pace. Finally reaching the register, Vincent takes out his black wallet to pay. I pause, noticing a pulse in his neck as he hands over his credit card for the cashier to swipe.

I stop smiling.

He looks worried and anxious, brows lowered in that dark and brooding way of his.

"Vincent," I touch his arm, "I'm here, okay?"

A line has formed behind us, but I couldn't care less. He swallows hard, the scruff on his face thicker than a few hours ago. Under the bright lights and white walls, his eyes are practically savage. "Don't want to waste time," he whispers with his teeth clenched, grabbing the back of my neck possessively as if he can't help it. I'm struck again by my tiny size compared to his. His grip isn't painful, but still, it's strong. The cashier looks at us nervously as the line grumbles in annoyance.

I focus only on Vincent, nodding gently in understanding. Stepping against him, I remove his hand from my neck and loop our fingers together.

"I'm still here," I swear. "We'll talk about everything later, okay?"

He nods and visibly relaxes before finally taking the plastic bag from the cashier.

We ride another ten minutes to his home. Pulling up to the side of his trailer, he lifts me off the bike and doesn't put me down until I'm on my back. I grab his soft sheets, fisting them as my body reignites. He moves to his knees, pulling me into his chest with so much emotion it steals my breath.

He's everywhere. Eyes closed. Licking and sucking at my neck so deep, marking me how I know he loves. A few beats.

"I'm gonna fuck you now, yeah? Can't wait anymore." His voice is desperate, our mouths melded.

"Please, Vincent. Yes," I whisper into his lips, wrapping my legs around his waist.

He enters me, groaning. "You're fucking gorgeous. Goddamn." He pushes in and out again, harder still, settling himself inside me and staking claim. Picking up one of my legs, he throws it over his wide muscled shoulder. My eyes practically roll back as he hits that spot so precisely; every inch of my body clenches tight, coiling. Bending down, he brings his mouth to my ear.

"Only me and you. Forever. Got that?" he growls, swiveling his hips in circles and grinding down on my clit. I'm moaning—out of my mind. Like a fire, the flames rove straight through me and down into my toes until they curl up in sweet agony.

Before I can catch my breath, he pulls me on top of him. I bring myself up and down on his cock, so slow. He's buried so deep, it's almost painful. So fucking good. He's cursing, begging me now.

Holding my hips with his hands and watching me fall down on him over and over again. We're drunk on each other. His grip tightens as he finally moves me the way he needs, grinding me down hard before raising me up again. My heart is about to beat straight out of my chest; pleasure mixing with emotional openness giving me a sublime high.

"Vincent," I moan, my voice hoarse.

The thought crosses my mind—if he ever left me again, I'd die. Vincent turns me desperate. He makes me *insane*. I drop my head down into the crook of his neck.

"Fuck," he groans, squeezing my hips hard enough to bruise as he presses me down harder and not letting go until he fills me to the brim.

My entire body is like lead in his arms, heavily sated. He slowly runs his calloused fingers over my skin, as if he can't bear not to touch. With his large hands, he cups my breasts and slides his fingers along my curves, humming deep in appreciation. I lay soundlessly, letting him take his time. Overcome by emotion, I find myself swallowing back tears. I never thought—

"Eve," he says, interrupting my internal voice.

"Yeah?"

His hand spans around my throat. He's gentle and yet, I'm completely at his mercy. "Never letting you go. Never," he commands. I know Vincent is dominant, always in charge. It isn't because of who his father is. And it isn't because he was raised in the Borignone mafia. It's just something within him. Anywhere Vincent goes, he's the king.

I lift my eyes to his, submitting. We wrap ourselves back up in each other until our lips are numb, all thoughts of the world around —my office, my shitty coworkers, our past—silenced.

The clock ticks and the sun begins to set. I turn, pressing his hand between my thighs. The room glows.

"We should talk about that night."

"Not yet. First, I want you to tell me about lockup. Let's start there." My voice comes out in a whisper. I want to know.

17

VINCENT

All she does is ask, and within seconds, I'm opening up about the worst time in my life. At first, it's as if I'm telling someone else's story. But somewhere between explaining the Boss Brotherhood and the look in her eyes, acute anxiety settles in my chest. I open my mouth to continue, but my throat is uncomfortably dry.

Sensing the change in me, she kisses my shoulder before hopping off the bed. I hear kitchen cabinets opening and the sink turning on. She comes back to me with a tall glass in hand, full to the brim with water. I drink the entire thing in one swallow.

After taking the glass from me and setting it on the side table, she curls up into my chest like a kitten. I press my forehead against hers, keeping our lips separated by mere centimeters. Her breaths enter my mouth, and it gives me strength.

"Prison. It was worse than you think. I did horrific shit without blinking an eye. Luckily, after I stood my ground with the B.B., everyone knew who I was. They all stayed back. Still. I-I don't know what to tell you. It was like there was a constant war on—" I stop, unable to manage. I know I have to talk to her about everything, and I want to, but it's too fuckin' much and I wasn't expecting this kind of emotional onslaught. She puts her hands on my shoulders. So gentle. So perfect.

"We have sex and now I'm unraveling." I laugh, but we both know it's not funny.

She pulls back, touching two scars in my left eyebrow. Moving her hands down my body, she lets her fingers graze over all my new wounds, pausing at the deepest one in my lower abdomen. We are both silent, but her eyes fill with pain at the sight.

"Oh my God, Vincent," she says, her face distressed. Fingers moving downward, she finds the stab wound in my thigh.

"Look at me," I say with as much strength as I can muster. "Things were bad. But they're over now."

"But how can you be so sure your father really let you go?" She's shaking her head from side to side, wild hair framing her face. "You said it once—no one leaves without a body bag."

"Believe it, Eve. I left and I'm still alive."

She moves closer, melting into me. But I'm not done with her—not yet. I move off the bed and drop down to my knees.

"Vincent, wait—"

"Don't deny me. I need to drink you in." I immediately slide my tongue inside of her, and she lets out a low moan. Time ceases to exist. Stopping myself isn't an option. I need to lose myself in her.

"Vincent. It's too much," she begs. God, she tastes so fucking good. I keep up my pace until her entire body is pink, flushed and shaking. She liquefies into my mouth and I savor every drop. When she's finished, I kiss back up her body and bring her to my chest. She fits.

"Eve, I need you."

"I know. I'm here." Love shines from her voice. But encasing her emotion is strength.

18

EVE

I clutch onto Vincent's back as we ride up the bright highway, nothing but open road and mountains ahead of us. The last forty-eight hours have been spent watching TV and alternating between fucking like crazy and making slow, savory love. We didn't talk much—we just *lived*. I'm not ready to open up about how he left me before prison. Discussing the details would only ruin this moment. Still, I'm worried that if we get into the past, everything between us will break down. Maybe I'm falling back into an old habit, but I trust we'll figure it out when the time is right.

He grilled steaks and corn for us every night, and I always made a big salad. I wanted to cook more for him, but he didn't want me busy in the kitchen. Doing work for the Milestone was nearly impossible, but we managed to get a bit done while tangled up in each other.

With Vincent, it's that mind-body connection. He takes me over on every single plane.

His home is tiny and perfect and we agreed that more than this just isn't necessary. What a relief not to deal with anything material. We have each other, delicious food, and a safe, warm home. What else is there? Over coffee this morning, he mentioned building us a house with a backyard one day—when we have kids.

I had burst into tears. He got down to his knees, holding me tightly around the waist. Not talking. Pulling off our clothes. Making love to me on the floor of his kitchen, cold tile becoming click with our sweat.

Gripping him as the wind whips around us, I let myself imagine our future. Vincent. Three children. A son and two daughters, because every girl deserves a sister. I hope they have his eyes. I want them to have his heart and strength too.

Our bike pulls into a dirt and cement parking lot, kicking up dust as we take a corner spot. Staring up, I see a huge red, white, and teal neon sign: THE BLUE. With nothing other than a gas pump and a handful of motorcycles, I'm equal parts excited and nervous. This life isn't what I'm used to, but still, it feels like it's where I'm meant to be.

Walking into the dimly lit restaurant and bar, country music plays on the speakers as I tightly clutch Vincent's hand. Being next to him fills my heart with pride—this brilliant, handsome, strong man is mine. I finally look around, eyes widening in surprise; the bar resembles an old New York City deli counter.

"This place is one of the few around here that's typical America." He walks us to a small booth in the center of the restaurant.

"Are most of the people here locals?" I sit down across from him, placing my hands on the table for him to hold; he immediately takes them.

"Yup. Believe it or not, most of the people here are Native Americans, but there's a range of blood degrees from full-blooded to practically blond, yeah?"

I gaze around the room and stare at the other patrons before settling back at the man in front of me, whose dark eyes haven't left my face. I flush, thinking about an hour ago when he was on top of me, going deep and slow.

Sexually, we're explosive. But it's so much more than that, and it always has been with him. I've known Vincent from when I was a little eighteen-year-old in the Blue Houses. The man took me for pizza and ice-skating, for God's sake. No one knows me like he does —so fully.

But I'm no longer a kid, and the realization is worrying. I'm a level-headed woman with a job and an apartment with a mortgage; my life is set on a track. But where does that leave us? The last few days have been spent in a dream world. Now we're out of his trailer and at a restaurant with the real world upon us. Our past—we'll deal with. But what about tomorrow? What about my work and the life I built? Anxiety brews.

19

VINCENT

She's stressing; I can see it in her eyes and in the tiny crease in her forehead. I'm done with tiptoeing around. There's no way I'm going to stop myself anymore around her.

"Come here," I say. I need to feel her, and she needs to feel me, too. Smiling with a little hesitance behind her eyes, she stands up to come to me. Before she can make another move, I grab and pull her into my lap.

"Vincent!" She giggles. I throw my arm around her shoulders as she nestles herself into my side. Her life gives me mine.

As much as I love disappearing from the world and staying in bed all day with Eve beneath me, I don't want to hide her like I had to back in college. Never again.

"We've gotta really talk now, babe." My voice comes out like gravel.

Her body shivers as I press my lips to her collarbone, snaking out my tongue to get a taste. So sweet.

The waitress comes over. "Hi! Do y'all know what ya want?" Her smile turns down as she stares at us with a look of confusion and nerves and I try not to laugh out loud. My girl is fresh with clear skin and shining eyes. So tiny and right now—cute as fuck with her hair in a high ponytail. Meanwhile, I've got my resting murder face, tatts, and four-days-worth of dark stubble.

Eve stares up at me, all trusting and innocent without any care that people are judging us. She's too good to me. Too good for me. Jesus Christ, *this woman*. I move an errant hair from her forehead before turning back to the waitress, asking for a few good things on the menu I've eaten before and think she'll like. Eve cuddles closer, letting me take care of her.

The waitress leaves, giving us privacy once again.

"So, when should I come back?" Her voice is whisper soft. She moves her nose to my shoulder, inhaling. "If you want me to nego- tiate some agreements for you, I can probably stay long—"

"Eve," I laugh, cutting her off. "I don't just want to hire you. Hiring you and your brilliant mind would be a perk. I want you in my bed every night." I rub the back of her neck as I stare into her eyes. She's hesitant, but still, she's going to have to hear this.

"I've been to hell and back, just as you have. I've got scars. And the truth is, my days of living in big-city luxury are behind me. I like the simpler life without all the goddamn noise. I'm happy with cash in the bank and you on the back of my bike. I'm not a clean-cut doctor. I've been in lockup. I've got a laundry list of sins." I pause, noticing she isn't panicking. I drop my hand on her thigh.

"I ran you from New York and ruined your life. No one knows it better than me. You need to hear now how sorry I am." I swallow. "But I couldn't drag you into that shit, and I think you know there was no other way to make sure you were safe. I also didn't want you coming out here and wasting your life waiting for me. But now I'm back, and I want you. Need you. Fucking love you babe and always have. It's time you move here with me."

20

EVE

The waitress returns carrying plates, interrupting Vincent from his speech. I take a minute to contemplate his words as the food is set in front of us. But with each passing second, I feel my temperature rise. We've been stuck in our own cocoon for days. But reality just punched through my door.

"Am I just your puppet?" He tilts his head to the side as if he's confused. "Is my life something you can control at your discretion?" The updated version of myself rears its head.

His eyes soften as he shakes his head. "No, it was never like that. It's still not like that. In fact, I need to tell you the truth about that night—"

I put up my hand, silencing him. "Tell me you're joking," I say angrily, pushing one of the plates away from me. A minute ago, we were drenched in love. He seems surprised by my hurt, but what can he expect? I'm still aching and it's not ignorable. "Forget college for a moment. Did you consult me before showing up at my office? Nope. You just came and stomped on my emotional well-being and sanity. Meanwhile, it's been seven years, Vincent. Seven fucking years."

I can feel my heart racing with an avalanche of emotion. "You waltzed into my office and threw millions at my firm—the one I worked my ass off to have a desk at—and I'm supposed to leave everything I've studied and worked for and come running back into your arms?"

We've been loving each other so hard the last few days, but with his admission, all of my resentment bubbles to the surface.

He pulls on the ends of his hair. "You have no idea the hell I was enduring in lockup, huh? I called you the second I got out and you didn't answer your fucking phone." His eyes flash.

"You knew where I lived, Vincent. You could have shown up to my apartment. But no, you had to come through work?"

"Hold up." He shakes his head, as if I'm not understanding him. He looks frustrated. "I only did that because I thought it would be a more comfortable way for you to—"

"—And you think I don't know what you must have gone through in prison? You threw me away." My voice breaks. I can't stop the words even if I wanted to. "I died for you, Vincent. Without you, I wasn't functional. I was basically s-suicidal." I squeeze the napkin in my fist, remembering my younger self wading into the ocean. Everything around me turns into a blur as pain slams into my bloodstream. The look in his eyes was cold. A girl on her knees before him. The imagines flash, turning my stomach.

He grabs the back of my head with his hand, keeping me tethered to him. "Well, I lived for you, Eve." His hold tightens, but I feel stricken. "I went through hell and back, and your face kept me alive. I told you all those years ago I would never be done with you. That I'd kill for you. Die for you. And baby? I'm no liar. You can be scared right now. You can be nervous. You and me, Eve, we'll never be over. And now that shit is finally clear out here, you're deluding yourself if you think I'll ever walk away from you again." He takes a sharp inhale through his nose. "I hurt you. I know it." His head moves up and down, once. "It was for your own good. And if as an adult, you can't see that? Well, you n—"

I let out a loud sarcastic laugh. "You don't get a choice anymore. I'm leaving here tonight."

"Leaving?" The word falls out of his mouth with surprise.

"Yes. I'm going." I throw my hands up. "You can't just expect me to uproot my life. I've built a whole world out in California. Working my ass off at work to make partner. And anyway, I think it's only a few more years away—"

"Fuck them," he presses his lips together, voice vibrating. "Come here and open your own law firm. Or don't. You love the Kids Learning Club. The teenagers on the rez could use your help, too. Half of them drop out of school and unplanned pregnancy is rampant. You could start a tutoring center."

"You can't just decide this for me." I turn my face around to see if we've garnered any attention. Luckily, the place is filled with patrons and the music is loud, drowning out our words.

He grips my hand in his. "I'm not blind. You hate working for that dickhead. And they treat you like shit, too. Let me guess, you think it'll get better? You can prove them all wrong?" His voice is accusing. "They harass you in that office, babe. I hate how you stay there. You need to quit that place. Now's a good time."

I sit back, pulling my hands away as if I've been slapped. He's so honest and accurate in his assessment that it momentarily jars me. "You have no right throwing that back in my face. I can deal with the way they treat me. I'm not weak." I grit my teeth.

"Of course, you're not. You're as strong as they come. But you don't have to eat shit in order to prove strength." He looks up at the ceiling as if to gather himself. "Okay. You need more time. Fine. Go back to L.A., a city I despise, and we'll do the long distance. That's what you want? Once or twice a month? Fuck like crazy before returning to some cold apartment? Newsflash. That's not the life I want and it isn't what you want, either. We've been separated long enough. That shit's gotta be done now. It's time." His voice is urgent.

"No," I shake my head from side to side. "No, it's not time. If I can just work for a few more years, I'll finally—"

"—make partner? And then what? So, you can continue as a cog in their bullshit machine? We both know it's not your calling. Yes—be a boss. But not there. Not for them."

"Don't say that," I gasp. "Don't come here and step all over my life and my work." I cross my arms over my chest, trying to stabilize myself. He's speaking truth, but it's butting heads with what I've been telling myself for years. It's too much.

"I'm not stepping on you, babe," he replies, his voice calmer. Gentle, almost. "You should have more than what they're giving you. You want to keep doing contractual work, I'll pull my money from Jonathan and give it all to you. The Milestone is yours. Do you hear me? Everything that's mine was yours and still is yours." His words are promises. I believe him. "I'm the one who messed up and lied to you. But come be with me now and let me make it right."

I drop my head down low, staring at the white-tile floor. Vincent puts his thumb under my chin to lift it back up before staring into my eyes. "If you don't want to do law anymore, just stop. I'll support anything you choose. You don't have to keep running to reach some goal you don't even care about. I know you, Eve. I know the real you. Real Estate law isn't your end game."

I touch my forehead, feeling totally out of sorts. I have no idea what it is I even want. I've been dreaming of this career for so long. Even if law in this capacity makes me miserable, it's all I've focused on. And now, am I supposed to just let it go? How can I?

I lick my lips, facing the window in the back of the restaurant. "This is too much, too soon. We just started seeing each other again. We haven't even talked enough about the past. And you've obviously thought all the details through. But I haven't."

"The past? It's simple. I staged the party to make sure you moved on. I wanted you safe and free. If anyone knew we had ties? If anyone knew you were mine? The backlash would have been a hundred times worse than what Daniela gave you. You'd be dead by now, Eve. My father alone was enough of a threat. Everyone had to know we were done. I didn't have a month to convince you to leave me. It had to be hard."

He puts his hand back under my chin, forcing me to look at him.

"Do you love me, Eve? Because you're the breath in my prayers. In my mind, it's only ever been *us*." His hands dig into my hair, gentle yet dominant, as his dark eyes fill with so much adoration, it stops my heart. "Do you love me?" he repeats.

I blink, the answer sitting on my tongue. I'm afraid to say it now. I'm scared of what it'll mean and what I'll have to give up. He waits, staring at me searchingly. Pleadingly. When he realizes I'm not replying, he sits back, looking knifed.

"I just need some time, okay?" My words fall out in a rush. "Let me go back to L.A. and just, s-sort it all out."

He lifts his hand, asking for the check as our entire meal sits untouched before us. Before the waitress can bring it over, he drops a few twenties on the table and stares at me expectantly, waiting for me to move from the booth. I feel like crying. Screaming. Telling him to just... hang on and wait, dammit! But Vincent waits for no one. It's who he is and why he's so successful. But right now? I'm the one getting stomped by his drive.

I move out of his way. He wastes no time in striding out of the restaurant, people stepping left and right to avoid getting run over by this beast of a man. He pushes through the front doors and I run behind him. I'm so mad, but still...

"Vincent, please—" I beg, practically chasing him to his bike.

He drops the helmet on my head, closing it tightly while refusing any eye contact. Climbing on, he waits with a look of impatience for me to join him.

Our entire drive is cold. I grip his waist as tightly as I can, wishing that somehow, I could open his brain and pour my feelings into him so he could understand.

Stopping in front of my hotel, he lifts his helmet. "Don't burn your legs when you get off." His words aren't said cruelly, but they are final. He's mad. He's so fucking mad.

Shakily, I climb off, trying not to crumble onto the ground as he rides away, leaving nothing but dust in his wake.

Fifteen minutes later, I'm still standing in the spot he left me—my body in a trance. Is Vincent gone?

* * *

I finally return to my hotel room. Packing my clothes and checking out is taking longer than expected.

Sitting on the white couch in the hotel lobby, I barely notice a single thing other than the desert, dimmed to gray by my sunglasses. This is exile.

"Miss?" One of the hotel staff touches my shoulder politely. "Your car is here for you."

I turn around, noticing a long black Escalade waiting in the hotel's driveway. I stand, walking out the sliding glass doors while the bellboy carries my bags.

The driver runs around the car, opening my door. I step in. Slade is here. He looks happy at first, but his mouth quickly turns down at my demeanor. I pull my sunglasses back over my eyes; the last thing I need is to talk to someone on Team Vincent. Taking a seat in the third row, I stare out the window, doing my best to avoid any conversation. Luckily, he stays silent.

Halfway to the airport, I sit up, pushing my glasses on the top of my head as an idea takes shape in my head.

"Sir," I call to the driver, clearing my throat. "Can you take me to the main airport, please?"

Slade turns around. "The private jet is ready for you." He sounds confused.

"I want to go to the regular airport," I repeat with as much strength as I can muster. "I no longer want to go back to L.A. I need to get to New York." My voice comes out strong and determined, and as words leave my lips, I feel an immediate sense of relief—as though I'm doing right.

I have a weekend before work Monday morning, and I want to go home—my real home—and sort this out. I actually believe every word Vincent said, but I need confirmation and answers from someone other than him. Angelo is in New York. It's time I hear the truth straight from his lips.

Not least, I'm sick and tired of running away from my past. It wasn't until I saw Vincent again that I realized how much pain I was carrying. Until I clear it up, I can't move forward with my life the way I need. I grip my purse, bringing it to my chest as I try not to bawl.

21

EVE

LaGuardia is gray and cold. Within twenty minutes of landing, I'm sitting in the back of a yellow cab telling it to take me to Seventy-Fifth Street and Second Avenue.

I enter Janelle's boutique hair salon, smiling wide, all of her white chairs are filled with clients getting cuts, color, and blow-dry. The place evokes a cool downtown style with 90s supermodels like Christie Brinkley, Claudia Schiffer, and Naomi Campbell gracing her walls in oversized black-and-white prints.

The salon is located uptown and designed to cater to rich girls who don't want their hair done by their moms' snooty colorists. I smile, trying not to roll my eyes at these teenagers and early twenty-somethings scrolling their phones, probably checking out the latest social media posts while having their hair brightened blonde. As Janelle likes to joke, these little shits are the ones paying top dollar for her services. So, as far as she's concerned, God bless 'em!

Before the girl at the front desk—who looks more model than human—can ask me who I'm seeing today, Janelle comes barreling toward me from the back of the salon.

"You bitch! You came without telling me!" she squeals, jumping up and down and throwing her arms around me. "How was Nevada? Ohmygod you look gorgeous!" She takes my hand, dragging me to the couch by the door.

We sit with our knees touching. She's still the light to my dark. The free spirit to my seriously focused.

"It was cool," I start. "I got a lot done—" I open my lips to continue, but the words catch in my throat as tears gather in the corners of my eyes. She encases me in a warm hug. Janelle smells like a floral vanilla. It's different from her usual scent, but it's still my sister.

Letting me go, I take a hard swallow as she pulls the clip from my hair. "You need a haircut." She grins. "I love it long like this, but let me trim your ends. I know we've got a shit ton to talk about, but everything will be better with good hair and some wine."

I can only nod, afraid that if I even try to speak, I'll cry. Luckily, Janelle knows this by just looking at me. "Quick wash first. I'll squeeze you between clients." She turns around, raising a hand in the air.

A young girl with a white crop top and pink streaks in her platinum hair comes running to us nervously. "Yes, Janelle?" She bites a glossy pink lip.

"Hi, Angeline. Wash. Two shampoos." Janelle's voice is commanding as she stares at the girl in that no-nonsense New York way. I missed this and can't believe how long it's been since I've been here. I'm quickly escorted to a chair in front of a small white sink. Once seated, Angeline places a warm towel behind my back—a nice touch.

The water turns on and I try and relax. The moment she scrubs my scalp with her fingertips, I have to try not to moan out in pleasure. Holy shit but this girl can wash!

Finally sitting in Janelle's stylist chair, Angeline taps my shoulder. "Can I bring you a coffee or tea? We have cappuccino, latte, regular, and decaf. Teas include green, black, and chamomile."

I turn to Janelle, smiling at her as if to say—damn girl, you did well!

"I'll take a cappuccino. Skim, please," I ask politely.

She walks away as my sister begins trimming my ends. Janelle tells me it's called *dusting*. "Hopefully you won't notice any change in length, but the hair, in general, will have bounce and freshness."

There's so much I want to tell her. I open my mouth to start.

"Just sit tight for now, okay? Let me do your hair. Tonight, when I'm home, we'll talk. I'm assuming this is about Vincent, right?" She shakes her head in anger.

I pull out my e-reader and open up an old favorite, reveling in the comfort of a good book while my sister takes care of me. I can be the big boss all I want in L.A. But within a second of being near Janelle, I'm back to being the baby. I would expect that feeling to annoy me, but it doesn't.

Forty minutes later, she tells me to lift my head and take a look. My hair is shining; dark waves fall down to the center of my boobs. I feel like...me.

She hands me a set of keys. "Go to my apartment. I'll be there around eight."

"I may go see Angelo early tonight." I step in for a hug.

"He's going to be thrilled. Always complaining that you never come home." She raises her eyebrows accusingly.

"Yeah, I know." Guilt rises up. It's been seven years since I've been back to the city. If Janelle hadn't come to visit, I probably never would have seen her. But, I'm here now.

I tip Angeline as she hands me my luggage. Walking the few blocks to Janelle's apartment, I let my mind wander to Vincent.

Deep in my gut, I know that he's right about my work. I'd be happier doing something that actually helps people. It's not as if real estate transactions were ever my dream. In fact, it came to me by happenstance. A friend in law school mentioned that Crier, the best firm in Los Angeles, was hiring. I went ahead and applied. When they offered me a job in their real estate department, I felt like—how could I turn it down? The money was phenomenal and it was so well known. So, I said yes. And now, here I am.

Using my legal degree to actually benefit the world is obviously more my speed. But I couldn't do it just because Vincent said so. Can't he see that? This is something I've got to think about for myself. I've spent the last however-many years of my life planning to be a lawyer; making partner was always the big goal. And it's so close, I can smell it. Sure, it's nothing like I thought it would be. And Vincent's not wrong that I'm unhappy. Still, it was always "the plan." Truthfully, I'm not even sure why making partner is so important. I can continue practicing law in a different capacity, and like he said, be my own boss.

Finally getting to Janelle's, I take the elevator up to the third floor and walk down the narrow hallway to apartment 6B. The space is a small one-bedroom, overlooking a courtyard with a wooden bench and patchy grass. It's not fancy, but it's just right—so much warmer than my apartment back in L.A.

A small photo of us hangs in her hallway; it's the two of us on the Blue Houses' stoop making kissy faces to the camera. I smile in surprise, having no idea she had this picture. We look so young. My baggy sweatshirt reaches my knees. God, I've come a long way. We both have.

I drop my things in the corner of her blue and white bedroom and pull out my phone from my purse. Disappointment ravages through my chest; he still hasn't called. Of course, he hasn't. I tried not to compulsively check my phone, but now that I've broken the seal, I'll probably be staring at it every other second.

Dialing Angelo, I let him know that I'm home. He's surprised, but also excited. I ask him to meet me for dinner tonight at a small Italian place I noticed on my walk over to Janelle's. We agree on six o'clock.

* * *

The restaurant is warm and cozy, complete with interior red-brick walls and candles lining the white-clothed tables. I scan the nearly empty room, finding Angelo at a table in the back corner. Walking toward him, he stands to greet me. We talk regularly, but I haven't seen him face to face since he brought me out to California. To my relief and happiness, he still smells and looks the same. Red and blue striped shirt and dark slacks. Aqua de Gio cologne. I couldn't stop my smile if I tried.

After a long and drawn-out hug, I take my seat across from him.

"Look at you! Fancy and gorgeous," he says with pride, lifting up a cup of tap water and taking a sip.

"Oh, please." I shake a hand in front of my face dismissively. "You know I just clean up well."

I took my time getting dressed this evening by putting on my makeup as meticulously as I could and choosing the classiest outfit in my suitcase. I guess I just wanted to show Angelo that I really and truly changed my life. Maybe I also wanted to prove it to myself.

My white button-up shirt is sheer, but not see-through. With my jeans in Janelle's washer, I opted for a pair of tan straight-leg trousers and nude Louboutin round-toe pumps.

"I missed you, doll," he tells me earnestly, his eyes crinkling in the corners. Finally, I notice the guilt swimming in his eyes. I swallow hard, knowing in my gut what's about to happen.

"Angelo," I start, clearing my throat. "I'm here for a reason." The waiter steps over, dropping a basket of bread and a small plate of olive oil in front of us. We both look up to thank him before he walks away.

"I figured." He shrugs sadly as if he has an inkling of what I need to discuss. "Talk to me." With elbows resting on the table, he shortens the distance between us.

"Well, I've seen Vincent." I stop to gauge his reaction—he's surprisingly calm. "I've been helping him on the Milestone, as his attorney. And he hinted at some things about our past. So, I'm ready to hear it all from you. Because you know how much I love and trusted y—" my voice breaks. "And you swore over and over. You swore it, Angelo. And—"

He shakes his head, putting out a warm hand to cover mine. "I never wanted to hurt you." He speaks quickly, defending himself. "I just wanted to help. Vincent knew how close me and you were..."

Tears drip down my face as he finally tells the whole agonizing story, hands moving quickly through the air as he delivers the painful details. After so adamantly swearing to those lies all those years ago —that Vincent was cheating and a liar, he's shockingly forthcoming with the truth: it was all a sham. Then again, a lot of time has passed.

Finally, he stops. I stare at him in silence, noticing sweat beading on his forehead. It's clear no one wanted to propel the lie, but neither Angelo nor Vincent thought there was a better option. My life was on the line because of our relationship. I was too young, too in love, and too invested in Vincent to just walk away from him.

"I trusted you, though, Angelo. And Vincent, he could have spoken to me." I sniffle, dabbing the napkin under my eyes.

"Well, he told me he tried. But you weren't going to give up on him. I mean, shit. If you stuck around and people found out about you, it would have been bad. And if you left to Cali and promised not to contact him, but you waited for him, that would have been fucked-up too." He drops a heavy fist on the table. "How could he ask you to wait and give up your life? Plus, Eve, I was angry with him for takin' you. I felt that he took advantage. It wasn't fair—you finally got that school and deserved time to grow. Instead, he took you as his own. Hid you. I wanted you freed from him." He licks his dry lips and I can feel my face turn down. "Come on, doll, you were just a kid." He fidgets with his collar.

"Angelo, what me and Vincent had wasn't just some small little fling." I am angry and shocked that he would ever be so dismissive. "We were in love. Real love. The soul-shattering, once-in-a-lifetime kind."

"But Eve, you were a baby. And so was Vincent. What's love between two kids? Losing your virginity under the stars?"

Shock moves through my insides, but he continues, backtracking to explain. "You know, that love that feels intense, but then you take time apart from each other and the dust settles and really, it was all just surface?"

I turn away and he shifts his chair, leaning closer. "I'm not saying it didn't feel serious, but I figured you were a lovesick child. Vincent is magnetic; we all know that. He's all brains and looks and power. I figured you'd leave and find someone else to take his spot. Someone who doesn't have gang connections for God's sake."

"You've got gang connections, Angelo, and I still love you. Or have you forgotten?"

"Doll, you know I fuckin' regret it every damn day. I was a kid when I got into it with the Borignones and now I'm stuck paying 'em and helping 'em 'til the day I die. They ruined my goddamn life. Did I want them to ruin yours, too?"

"No, Angelo," I exclaim. "But..." I pause. "Vincent and I may have been young. But we were real. We were honest and open and it wasn't about where we came from or who we knew; it was more than that. I love him for who he is beneath the exterior and he felt the same—" I stop, swallowing hard. Vincent loved the old me. And he loves the new me, too.

"We read books together," I add, my voice cracking. "We studied; he helped me in my classes. We laughed. We spent months just talking and eating and making love. We used to dance together in his kitchen because he knew how much I loved to dance. He brought me to his gym to learn MMA. He always empowered me—"

Like an avalanche, my feelings for Vincent hit me so hard, I'm practically floored by the force of it. I love Vincent. Why am I running from him? How could I even consider letting him go? He isn't trying to take my life away from me. He wants the best for me, still. I don't want to run anymore.

They lied, but both of them thought it was the only way. And outside of that, they've always been honest. I want to forgive.

I move my hair over to one shoulder, gathering myself. "Regardless, you had no right to lie, Angelo. No. Right. You played with my life."

He drops his head for a moment. "I'm sorry for the lies." His eyes move to mine, watering. "So many times, I wanted to apologize to you, doll. But I figured it was just water under the bridge. You became an adult and made it so far in life." He lifts his hands, gesturing to the new me. "Fancy job and decent boyfriends and that nice apartment. You stopped asking about him," he shrugs. "I thought you just moved on."

"But I didn't. I never did." Desperation tinges my voice.

"So, you think you still love him?" he questions.

I nod my head *yes*.

He stands, taking his brown wallet out of the back pocket of his jeans before sitting back down again. Opening the worn-in leather, he pulls something out. "This is yours. Vincent stopped by the pawn-shop and gave it to me before he went into lockup. Wanted me to hold it for you." I put out my hand as the thin gold chain collapses into my palm. A gold crucifix shines on top of the golden pile.

"I hung onto it 'cause it made me think of you. It's yours again, doll, if you want it."

My hand stays open, eyes trained on the necklace sitting in the center of my hand.

"H-he tells me he's out of the fold," I tell Angelo.

"Yup." He bunches a napkin in his hand. "I don't know all the details, of course. But I know Tom stepped up. Antonio ain't happy about it, either. It's all anyone talks about these days—how the prince left his throne." He lifts a hand, pushing his hair back. "Antonio's gotten a hell of a lot crazier, too, since Vincent left. Anyways, maybe you gotta give it another chance. No one's a kid anymore. If you still feel it with Vincent, who am I to say otherwise?"

The waiter comes to take our order, but my stomach is rolling; there's no way I can eat right now. "I have to go, Angelo. I need to call him." My chest squeezes as I finally clutch the necklace in my warm palm, swinging my head toward the door. Even if I don't know all the details of how we'll make it work, I can't walk away.

Angelo lifts his hand, telling me to wait. "And I'm sorry. With all my heart, doll, I'm sorry I lied. All I can say is I thought it was the right thing. For *you*." He opens both his hands to me, pleadingly.

"Okay. I'm going to go now though, all right?"

We stand up and hug before I hesitantly pull away. Dropping the necklace into the small zipper pocket of my purse, it now sits beside the silver boot charm that I never leave home without.

"Bye, Angelo."

"Always love you, doll."

I pull out my cell phone as I move to the door. I have to call Vincent—now. I need to hear his voice. He has to know I love him. I still don't have all the answers, but I can figure those out. He'll give me the time I need. He just needs to know I'm in this with him.

The city streets pass in a blur, tears clouding my vision as I run through the hectic blocks filled with people. Upper East Side moms push wide strollers with huge wheels. People returning from work are hustling to cross the street before the light changes. Rumpled suits wave down cabs. I forgot about the New York City hustle, and the feeling is both heart-pounding and claustrophobic. I practically trip over a kid scootering on the sidewalk in my haste to get to Janelle's faster.

The phone rings and rings, but Vincent doesn't pick up. Taxis honk like mad at a traffic jam ahead. One Starbucks turns into the fourth I've seen. Still, he hasn't answered. *Where is he?*

22

VINCENT

Thirty Minutes Earlier

I drop myself at the bar while Sam Hunt blares on the speakers, taking my phone out of my pocket and leaving it on the old bar top. I'm looking forward to getting completely hammered. I don't make a habit of it, but now that Eve basically told me she isn't ready to commit, I feel like this is the only viable option. My phone rings, blinking red. Checking the caller ID, I see it's Slade.

"Yo," I answer.

"Hey man. Where you at?"

I lift my chin to the bartender, trying to get his attention. "Come join me for some drinks. I'm at The Blue."

Turning my head around, I spot the table Eve and I were at just a few hours earlier. My stomach clenches. I should have found a different bar, but coming here is second nature at this point.

His voice comes out scratchy; I can barely make out his voice through the static. "Be the-r- la—" The line cuts out.

Christ, but I need to find a way to get better cell phone service out here. It's annoying as hell. Hanging up, the bartender moves in front of me. I order myself a Jack and Coke.

I finish my first drink when Slade drops into the seat next to mine.

"Dude, what the fuck happened? Eve ran off like she was heading to a goddamn funeral." He raises a hand and the bartender nods in acknowledgement. "Oh, and she didn't go to L.A."

"What the fuck you talking about?" I turn to face him.

"Dropped her off at the regular airport. She went to New York City."

"She must have gone home to talk with her sister. And Angelo." I grab my glass, squeezing it so hard my knuckles hurt.

"You gonna tell me what happened?" Slade asks before ordering his drink. I go through the general outline of events, ending with the shitty way I dropped her off in front of the hotel. Repeating it like this, out loud, makes me realize that I may have seriously fucked up.

"Listen, brother." He clears his throat. "She's worked pretty fuckin' hard to get where she is right now. You gotta understand that. You can't just throw it all at her and expect her to say *yes*."

My heart beats erratically. "You don't get it. I've waited for an eternity. And she hates her job, anyway. There's nothing out in L.A. for her. If she wants, she can do law out here, too." I sound like I'm making excuses, but still, it's the truth.

"Come on, man. That may be right, but it's gotta be a conversation. Not an edict."

"It's been long enough," I grumble. "If she wanted—" I close my mouth, dropping my head into my hands and pulling on the ends of my hair. "I should call her. Apologize again. Ask one more time if—"

"No. Just chill and let her work it out. She'll come to you when she's ready." He pats me on the back. "No doubt."

I exhale, long and slow. He's right. How could I have given her the cold shoulder after telling her to end her career? I went about it all wrong. I curse under my breath, rubbing my face. I'm goddamn impulsive. She didn't say she loves me, but I know she does. Of course, I know. I was supposed to go slow. But instead of keeping up that pace, I ran over her. I shake my head, angry at myself.

We drink together in silence until Slade stands up, dropping money on the bar. "Wanna head out?" he asks.

"Nah, not yet."

He leaves, and I continue to agonize.

I try to relax, bringing forward memories of Eve.

She's trying to sit up in bed, but I keep grabbing her waist, pulling her down to me.

"Vincent, I've gotta get to class!" She giggles. Again, she tries to get up, but I don't let her. Throwing her on top of me as if she were my own personal blanket, I wrap my arms around her back.

"Need you, babe," I grumble.

"And I need an A in Ethics." I can feel her smile against my chest.

I sink my teeth into her shoulder and she cries, "Ouch!" My tongue laves the mark. Love how she tastes. Even though I can't see her, I feel her epic eye-roll.

"I'll tutor you," I move my lips to her neck. "You'll get the A; I promise. Skip class."

She struggles to get free, but I only laugh.

"There's got to be a way to get out of your hold."

She's turning angry, and I love her angry face. I turn us around so that I'm straddling her. She lets out a huff of annoyance. I place my large hand around her wrists, locking them above her head. She immediately quiets.

"I'm not so sure that's possible. Seeing as I'm over a foot taller than you." I trail my palm down to the valley between her breasts, moving down the curves of her hips. "Much heavier than you, too." I let go of her hands as I lift her bottom half into the air, bringing myself to the edge of the bed.

"You never play fair, Vincent." She tries to maintain composure. As usual, she knows what I want. Her eyes are trained on me as I stare at her body hungrily, dragging her soft white cotton underwear down her thighs...

A blonde takes the seat next to me, interrupting my dreaming. "Hey," she says in a sweet voice.

I ignore her, wanting to go back to my daydream, but she introduces herself to me anyway. "I'm Emma."

Turning toward her, she places a small pale hand on my arm. I stare down at her fingers, ready to pry them off. Before I can, I look up at her and see her smiling. Eve runs into my thoughts and the way I treated her today. The last thing I should do is be a dickhead to some innocent girl. She's wearing a cardigan for fuck's sake.

"What are you drinking?" She turns red, seemingly embarrassed by her forward behavior. She lifts her fruity-looking cocktail to her mouth before continuing. "I moved here last year from Idaho. My grandfather lives on the rez." Fuck, she's trying to make small talk. I gulp down my drink and ask the bartender for another.

"I live in town now," she continues, taking another sip. "I'm a teacher at the elementary school. Third grade." She pauses, staring at me hard as though she's trying to place me. "Wait a sec—are you Vincent Borignone? The Milestone?" Her voice and eyes are starstruck.

"Yup," I nod.

Girl's got a strange glint in her eye, but she keeps talking as if I'm some goddamn celebrity. I continue to act like I'm listening, as though I were a decent guy.

I press my lips together. Fuck, but I miss Eve so badly. She's probably with Angelo and her sister right now. I should just call him. But I can't interfere any more than I already have. Slade's right, anyway. She has to decide this for herself. Still, it's hard to sit back and wait when I know that she'd be happier doing something else. Doesn't she know I would never take things away from her? I always have and always will put her first, and I know she'd do the same for me.

I want to shift in my seat, but somehow, I can't move. It's as if my arms and legs are paralyzed. I try to kick out my feet again, but they do not budge. *What the fuck?*

I stare at my phone on the bar. It's blinking red. I see Eve's name on the screen; she's trying to call. I want to answer, but my body is no longer taking direction from my mind. *What is going on here?* I only had a few drinks, not enough to get me hammered like this. Sweat breaks out on my forehead as nausea turns my stomach.

"He's Vincent Borignone. Just confirmed it." I hear Emma smugly talk to someone behind me.

"Crow's gonna be thrilled we got him so quickly. Nice job, sweetheart." From my side-eye, I see money exchanging hands before a pair of strong arms pull me off my stool. Two men I don't recognize, both wearing leather vests, hold me by the shoulders. I want to get free, but it's a losing battle. My head lolls to the side as they grip me, lugging me out of The Blue. I can vaguely hear them tell the bartender they're my friends, here to get me home safely.

Moments later, I feel the warm Nevada air, and my entire world goes black.

23

EVE

It's been over twenty-four hours of calling Vincent, but I can't get through to him. In my gut, I know something's wrong. He was angry and lashing out before I left. But after what he told me about the way he feels, I don't think he'd just stop answering. No. I know he wouldn't. I pace Janelle's small bedroom while she watches me with sadness in her eyes. She ordered sushi that's sitting in the kitchen, untouched. I can't eat.

I already spoke with Kimber, who can't get a hold of Vincent either. I called the number on the business card Slade gave me the day I came out to Nevada, but he also isn't answering.

I told Janelle all the details of what happened between me and Vincent. She hates him for everything he's put me through and swears she always will. Regardless, she's sitting with me as I stress out, and that has to be enough.

My phone rings and I answer without checking the caller ID. "Hello?" I pray to hear Vincent's voice.

"Eve. Something's up. It's Slade." His voice is clipped but calm.

"Is it Vincent?" I swallow, moving my free hand to my bottom lip.

"I've been trying to call him and he won't answer." My voice comes out in a rush. I can practically feel the mounting pressure in my head.

"You've gotta get out of New York tonight."

"W-why?" I stutter.

"There's a lot going on. Vincent's been taken, Eve. I'm sending a car right now to bring you to Teterboro airport. The jet will be waiting to—"

"Wait a second. Vincent's been taken?" I drop into Janelle's desk chair. "Where?"

I can hear his loud exhale over the phone. "I got a call from Tom. Turns out Antonio's anger over Vincent reached a crescendo. He hired the Boss Brotherhood to kill Vincent. They've got him now, most likely at their clubhouse in Nevada."

"But, why would he do that? Why would he—"

"—Tom tried to warn Vincent that Antonio was losing it, but he didn't want to listen. Antonio doesn't care about his son, Eve. Shit went south during the years Vincent was in lockup. And when Vincent came home and told his father he was backing out of the family, Antonio lost it."

Bile, like liquid acid, rises up my throat.

"You know the line, cut off your nose to spite your face?"

"Mmhmm," I manage to hum.

"Well, that's Antonio. He knows how important Vincent is for business. But he's mad, Eve. He's mad that Vincent walked away from him. Not because he gives a shit, but because no one walks away from Antonio Borignone. It's a loss of control. And to an egomaniac, nothing could be worse. Do you understand me? I'm sorry for rushing through this, but we don't have time right now. Vincent is in the hands of lunatics. You've gotta get him out of there."

"M-me?" My head spins.

"Yes. Antonio knows who I am and that I've got Vincent's back. The likelihood that the BB knows my face and that I'd be coming for Vincent is high. But you—you're unknown."

Janelle bends her knees to come face to face with me. "What's going on?" she mouths.

I widen my eyes and shake my head at her, but don't reply.

"I'm going to email you details so you can study on the ride over," Slade adds.

"What?"

"I was able to put together a map of the clubhouse. If you go in there as a girl looking for a wild night, there's a chance you can get into one of the bedrooms and then into the basement." His voice is confident, leaving no room for negotiation; this is Slade in his natural element, military training on point.

I turn my head to the floor, staring at the silver diamond pattern on the carpet.

"Eve?" His voice is urgent. "You in?"

My breath exits my mouth slowly as I gather my wits. If I go in there, I'll be risking my life. But without Vincent, there is no life. And regardless of the drama and pain of our past, I would never turn my back. Could never. No amount of self-knowledge and reflection can change the outcome of my choice because—Vincent.

"Okay," I respond, my mind made. "Send the car. I'm at Janelle's on—"

"I know where you are."

I hang up the phone. "Well?" Janelle asks curiously.

"Vincent's been taken." My voice comes out shaky as our eyes lock. "I'm going back to Nevada tonight. He's at some motorcycle clubhouse right now. Slade wants me to go in there and get him out, but I have to look like a girl there for the party. He has a plan—"

She raises her hand in the air, cutting me off. "Oh, fuck you Vincent Borignone!" she screams to the ceiling before training her angry gaze back on me. "You can't risk your life for his, Eve. I'm not letting you go."

"Janelle," I reply quietly. "I love him—"

"Love shouldn't mean that. Love shouldn't bring you down or kill you, for God's sake. And Eve, take a look at yourself. Nothing about you spells *club slut* looking for a good time with bikers."

"I'll figure it out—"

"No. I'm coming with you. You'll need help turning yourself into one of these girls and that's something I can do." Janelle jumps off her bed and immediately takes out a small duffle from her closet shelf and drops it onto the floor. Gathering her makeup cases from the bathroom, she places them into the bag before running back into her closet and removing clothes.

She pauses, turning back to me. "Pack your shit, Eve. And call that fucker, Slade. Tell him that I'm going to need his plane to bring me back here when I'm done with you. I've got appointments I can't miss."

"Janelle, I can't ask this of you. It's too much. It's too risky. I don't even know all the details—"

"The only one at risk right now is you. You're my sister. I'll be there to help you get ready and I want to see you walk out of there in one piece. Maybe I'll even come inside with you. Afterward, I'll come back to New York. As much as I despise Vincent, I love you more. If you're gonna do this, I'm there."

We leave the apartment together, taking the emergency steps to the lobby. The street corner is quiet. Minutes later, a black Escalade pulls up to the curb.

Janelle takes my hand and squeezes three times—our version of a promise. The tinted window opens. "Eve?" The driver's eyes dart from Janelle to me.

Without replying, Janelle opens the back door and climbs inside; I step in right behind her and shut it with a forceful *slam*.

24

VINCENT

When I come to, I find myself on my knees in a dark and rank holding cell. My black T-shirt sticks to my skin, heavy and cold with salty sweat.

Moving my arms proves impossible; I seem to be connected to the wall behind me—the cuffs and chains feel like hard iron as I try to maneuver myself. I attempt to tug and pull with all my might—but the handcuffs bite into my wrists, making me cringe. I stop, knowing it's useless. A lesser man may yell or scream, but not me. Licking my cracked and dry lips, I wait patiently for whomever it is to show himself.

Sometime later, the light flips on, temporarily blinding me. I want to cower from the brightness, but instead, straighten my spine. My knees cramp from the position, but I show nothing but strength. A group of men in identical leather vests saunter into the cell, the door shutting behind them when none other than Crow steps up to where I'm kneeling. I come face to face with his legs, covered in tattered blue jeans.

"Welcome to hell, Borignone. No crew to back you now. No fists, either." He grabs the roots of my hair and pulls upward until our eyes lock. His pupils dilate from excitement.

His jaw is still fucked up, courtesy of me from the prison yard. I try not to smirk.

"What do you want?" My voice is firm. I may be tied up and at his mercy, but I'll never show weakness. There are some things I can't unlearn; being unshakeable in the face of a threat is one of them.

"What do I want?" he repeats mockingly, shaking his head to his crew like I just asked the most ridiculous question on earth. As though it's happening in slow motion, he turns toward me and strikes his black boot straight into my stomach. I double over, but my chains keep me from collapsing.

Leather vests surround me—a move meant to intimidate. There is no longer a doubt that these men want my blood and suffering. But to what end? Information? Death?

"The question is, Vincent, why did your father call me a few days ago, requesting I kill you?"

Before I can process his words, his fist rears back and slams into my face once. Twice. Three times. My pain threshold heightens— brass knuckles. I can feel the warm blood pouring thickly down my face. I blink, trying to replay what I heard amidst the physical agony.

"Men like you have no goddamn morals. No code of ethics," he shouts close to my ear, spraying spit into my beaten face. "When we're done with you, MOTHERFUCKER, you'll wish you had your father to answer to instead of us. Your time is up." He's bouncing on the balls of his feet.

"The fact that I hate your guts and get to torture you before I kill you?" His laugh is slow and maniacal as he lifts his head to stare at the ceiling. "Bonus," he cries, his voice echoing around the small room. It doesn't take long for my eyes to swell shut. Darkness.

I hear the flick of a lighter before the smell of cigarettes hits my nose.

The hard butt of a gun slams across my face and more blood flows into my mouth.

I can feel music somewhere above; the bass pounds into the ceiling. I'm pushed forward until my arms are splayed straight. What feels like a hundred heavy boots begin kicking my back until I can barely inhale; my ribs are cracked.

The men pause, seemingly to take a break. Someone unceremoniously unchains me, and I crumble onto the cold ground. Her name pounds its way into my head. *Eve. She's my life*. Maybe my father will arrange to have her taken, too. I'm not afraid of my own death. But, I am afraid of hers. The idea of her dying is enough to take away my strength. Since I met her, she is the one who gives order to my life. Eve is stability amidst chaos.

I keep myself still, focusing my thoughts. "Please, Eve, forgive me. For everything I've done. Jesus, keep her safe." Nowhere other than with Eve have I ever felt peace.

I hear a *zipping* sound. My breath hitches as I feel a body step in front of me. I try to cling to the picture of her face, but my brain muddles from what is to come. She's sobbing in my arms after we made love on the floor of my office. Something slams down onto my knee—the *crack* shocks me until I see stars behind my eyes. I want to tell Eve not to cry, but she can't hear me. She's detaching. Am I screaming?

My stomach tightens and a smoke-like numbness spreads in my lower half until I can barely feel the blows.

I'm silent—checked out and taking the beating like the man I was raised to be. But when I feel the point of a sharp knife digging beneath my eye and carving its way down my neck, I roar.

25

EVE

Janelle and I sit in the back of Slade's blue pickup truck as he drives to the Boss Brotherhood clubhouse. According to two of Slade's friends, who recently surveyed the scene, the party is raging tonight.

"Okay, so you got it all now, Eve?" Slade asks for the hundredth time.

"Yes," I reply with confidence. I know he's worried about me right now. I'm hopped up on a ton of adrenaline and feeling like I can take on the world.

"The club whores should help you, got it? Those girls know all the ins and outs. Find them first and make nice. They'll point out the important guys. But don't look threatening or they'll never let you in." He sounds like a drill sergeant.

"Right," I respond at the quick.

Clutching my full purse like a lifeline, I remind myself that everything I need is safely tucked away in this bag—goodies courtesy of Slade—loaded pistol, sharp knife, a handful of condoms, and two vials of pentobarbital, according to Slade it's a common barbiturate that will incapacitate a man. Of course, I also have my phone, and per Janelle's orders, a tube of red lipstick to reapply if necessary.

On the flight over, Slade sent me an email complete with attachments of the clubhouse map along with a detailed plan that I've since sworn to follow to the best of my ability. Operating under the assumption that Vincent is in one of their holding cells in the basement, it's my job to go in and get him out of there.

"Slade," Janelle calls out. "Are you sure me or one of your friends can't go in, too? I don't like the idea of her being alone in there."

"No," he replies forcefully. "The party is closed to any men who aren't either part of the club or typical hang-arounds. And your presence may lessen her chances of finding Vincent. It's more likely the men will see Eve as easy meat if she's alone and without a friend."

I turn to Janelle, squeezing her hand. "I'll be okay. Don't worry."

Janelle sits back and purses her lips. I know she's angry and worried, but there is no room for negotiation.

Slade turns up the rock music, Papa Roach blaring on his speakers. We're speeding; no one is out on the road right now other than us. Still, I wish I could snap my fingers and just get there already.

The phrase "time is of the essence" pops up in my head, a line I've used millions of times at work in relation to parties signing contract agreements within a stated time. I start to laugh, thinking about how ridiculous it is that I ever thought anything in this life could be time sensitive. Compared to this, that part of my life feels like a joke.

Slade turns his head back and forth between the road and the back seat. "You hanging in?"

I laugh harder, tears dripping down my face like thick drops of rain. "I'm f-fine." I don't even try to hold in it—I can't. Unfortunately, this crazy nervous laughter is something I never completely grew out of.

"She does this sometimes. Annoying as hell," Janelle voices loudly. Slade lets out an awkward chuckle, but unfortunately, it does nothing to stop my hysterical laughter.

About twenty minutes later, we pull into the dark driveway of a wooden ranch house in The Middle of Nowhere, Nevada. I grab the small mirror from Janelle's handbag and take a good look at the woman staring back at me. I'm not recognizable, not even to myself: blood-red lips, dark-brown eyes rimmed heavily with coal-black liner, and heavy foundation, two shades lighter than my natural skin tone. Contouring has my nose looking miniscule and cheekbones razor sharp. There is no other way to describe my look except to say that I'm *changed*. I'm about to clean the black mascara that smeared below my eyes when Janelle grabs my hand.

"Don't touch it. You look like a girl down for *anything*—it's perfect." The anger in her gaze is gone and in its place is confidence. "You got this, girl. Navigating this shit is in your blood. It's time to channel it now."

The *click* of the door unlocking is my cue. I pause to compose myself.

"I'm ready," I tell them both, voice sure.

"I'll be waiting by the emergency door out back. Once you have Vincent, text me—"

"I know, Slade. Trust me."

I turn to go when Janelle pipes up. "Eve? You better come back. I'm waiting for you."

I nod solemnly before swinging the door open and jumping out. The weather is warm and balmy and the night sky sprinkled in stars. Rows of black motorcycles line the front of the clubhouse like a foreboding fence.

I strut toward the front door full of attitude, bringing forth Blue House-girl-on-the-stoop. My boobs pour out of my slinky red tank top and my skirt is so short, I'm sure any of these guys could see the underside of my ass.

Janelle's clothes were obviously what I needed for a night like tonight. If she didn't come with me and bring all this stuff, I'm not sure how I would have made this work. After I changed, she did my makeup in the back seat of the car. She even packed a pair of sandals, if you can call a pair of patent-leather six-inch spike heels with a platform, a sandal. Janelle explained the entire outfit and shoes was from a Halloween costume party a few years ago called "pimps and hoes." *Whatever*. My sister turned me into sex on legs tonight and nothing else would have done it. I'm sure our mom would be proud.

The front door is flanked with two youngish-looking guys wearing white T-shirts beneath black-leather vests. They scan my body and I seductively purse my lips while pushing my tits out, making a visual promise. Luckily, after their eyes get their fill, they step aside.

"Come on in," the taller one says, his voice heavily laced with a southern twang.

I strut by them and walk straight to the bar, the smell of stale beer assaulting me. Guns N' Roses' "Sweet Child O' Mine" plays in the background as goosebumps erupt on my arms; I know it in my bones that Slade is right—Vincent is here, somewhere.

I act as though I'm holding back a smile as men turn their heads, rubbernecking to get a good look at me. A huge wooden swastika painted gold and red, hangs on the wall. It catches my eye and sickens me, but also serves to make my mission more real.

Seven years have gone by without Vincent. College. Law school. One man. Other men. But my hope never completely died; there was always a sliver of faith that he'd come back. That he didn't lie. That our love was real. And now he's so close. I can't let him go again —I *won't*.

I lean forward against the badly damaged wood—the words WHITE POWER etched deeply within and sticky from spilled drinks. My stomach clenches and I send a silent prayer to Janelle, thanking her for the heavy makeup that's lighter than my olive skin.

Looking to my left, there is a blonde girl with hair in high pigtails next to me. She's wearing a triangle American flag bikini top and ultra-tiny jean shorts. An opened beer rests happily in her hand.

"You're new here." She takes a swig. "I'm Heather. How did you hear about the party?" She smiles kindly.

"Met one of the guys at the supermarket. Told me to come on down." I shrug, my New York accent nice and sharp.

"Ohmygod are you from New York City? I love it there! Not that

I've ever been, but it's always been my dream." She bounces up and down excitedly. New York City is always a big hit with girls like these.

I stare at Heather, who may be called beautiful—if not for a wide and deep scar running from her nose to her ear. She caked her makeup for cover, but it didn't work. Her eyes are genuinely kind, though.

"Where are you from?" I need to keep the conversation rolling.

"Oklahoma. But I haven't been back there in years." She lets out a small and awkward smile before taking another long sip. "I'm with Guns. He takes care of me."

I click my tongue. "I could use that too, if you know what I mean. Haven't exactly had an easy go of it lately." I drop my head for a moment, my voice down and out.

"Oh, girl, I've been there." She touches my shoulder in solidarity. "You see that guy over there in the green baseball hat?" She moves closer to me, bringing her voice to a whisper.

I scan the room and immediately spot him. "Yeah," I reply. "You mean the one standing under the swastika?"

"Yeah. Him. He's the treasurer. But all the girls say he's into some crazy kinky shit. You're not into that, right?"

"No. No way." I shake my head vehemently.

"Unless you're real desperate, I would skip him. The guy next to him? That's Crow." Both our eyes widen, but for different reasons. I recognize his name from what Vincent told me about his time in prison. "He's the president and the one to latch onto. Got out of lockup six months ago and I know for a fact he isn't interested in the club whores. He's always into new girls who haven't been touched by any of the other members." She's enthusiastic as if she likes the idea.

"Thanks, Heather." I smile wide. "I really hope he likes me."

"Oh, he will. You're exactly his type."

I stare at her a moment, wanting to take her by the hand and run her out of here. She's such a nice girl—and so young, too. She shouldn't be here.

"Oh!" she starts, interrupting my thoughts. "He's comin' over here. This may be your shot," she squeaks.

As luck would have it, the men move to my right. Heather takes that as her cue to leave.

"... bleeding out in the basement."

I inch closer, pulling out my phone and keeping my eyes trained on it while listening as keenly as my ears will allow.

"Let's head down in another hour or so. Let him sit in his own piss a while."

I hear a grunt that sounds like agreement. "Should we send one of the boys in there to watch him in the meantime?"

"Nah. No way in hell he can move." Dark laughter ensues.

My blood burns hot, but I don't freak out. Instead, I let out a breath of relief. My mind flickers to Vincent's face and I vow to be the greatest actress there ever was. That's my man they're talking about, *and he's alive.* I'm getting Vincent out of this hell hole.

Crow turns forward, presumably to order a drink. He rubs his forehead with his palm thoughtfully as I angle myself in a way so he can see me.

I catch his eye. Raising an eyebrow in appreciation and surprise, he takes a long slow look from my feet up to my face.

I smile, all coy, playing with Vincent's cross around my neck as I quickly read the patch on his vest for confirmation. Jackpot. Anger streams through me, but also something else—excitement. I want to take this asshole down. I loathe to think about the scar he gave Vincent in the yard, the story still making me ill.

He creeps up to my side and I give him another sexy smirk. He's tall. Not as tall as Vincent, but still big enough that I have to crane my neck up to see his face. Small brown eyes peer down at me through narrow slits, gazing as if I were a fresh piece of ass he can't wait to taste. His head is shaved smooth, showing bluish veins along pasty skin and a slightly crooked jaw. A dark swastika is tattooed on the front of his neck along with a set of numbers below. I feel a surge of hatred so strong, it outshines any possible fear.

I slide my tongue slowly across my front teeth, lips slightly parted, eyes trailing his body as though I like what I see. That's when I notice the collar on his white shirt is stained with what looks like blood splatter.

"Hey," he says in a raspy voice, leaning a tattooed forearm on the bar. His knuckles are bruised. "Having fun?"

"I am now." My voice is quiet enough to bring him closer. I need this to happen—quickly. There's no time to waste.

After a few seconds of eye contact, he turns his head. "Yo, Chub!" he yells to the big guy with a beard pouring people drinks. Chub immediately stops and turns to Crow, waiting for his command. "Natty Light," Crow simply states.

Chub's blue eyes widen before turning to a huge trash can and pulling out two beers, wet from condensation, and handing them to Crow.

"Glad you came tonight. Got a name?" He cracks a can, the *hiss* sharp and quick. I let my fingers cover his for just a moment before taking it for myself.

"Yeah. I've got one." My voice is seductive as I bring the drink up to my mouth nice and slow. There's noise all around us, but I'm completely focusing my attention on him. I want him to feel like a king right now.

"You gonna give it to me?" His thin lips quirk up.

"Depends on how badly you want it." I raise my eyebrows flirtatiously and he laughs out loud.

He moves closer to me. "Waiting, sweetheart. And a man like me doesn't like to wait. Even if it's from a sexy-as-fuck woman like you."

"Irina." My voice is soft as I look up into his eyes. The irony that I'm using my mother's name isn't lost on me.

"Crow."

I hum, the vibration fluttering around my lips.

His smile reaches his eyes. I can feel it—he actually likes me. "So, you ever ride?"

"Nope. I've always wanted to, though. Looks like fun." I cock my head to the side.

It's a few more minutes of small talk before he takes my hand and walks me out of the party, straight into the quiet white hallway where the bedrooms are located. I grip his damp hand tightly, as though I don't want to let go. He squeezes mine back, and I know I've got him just where I want him.

"Don't normally bring anyone back here." His voice is gruff.

Crow pushes open a door. Before stepping inside, I make a mental note that we're in the third room on the left. The light flicks on and I take stock of the situation. Queen-size mattress on a box spring pushed against the wall. Black sheets and two white pillows. A wooden cabinet in the corner with an old boxy TV perched on top. A small table in the corner.

We're alone.

The light is dim and yellow.

This is dangerous. Every internal alarm I have in my head is screaming for me to run. Not only is this man a complete stranger, but he has Vincent's blood on his shirt. Still, my heart tells me to stay clear and straight. Step one, get him relaxed. I go on hyper-focus, bringing forth everything I've got.

I purse my lips as my fingers lightly caress my breasts. I let my hands roam over my nipples; they harden under the thin fabric of my shirt. He grumbles like a pitiful dog.

"You want?" I'm all innocence.

"Fuck yeah," he grunts, voice hoarse from desire. Unbuckling his belt, he pulls down his blue jeans, kicking off his ratty black boxers next. Sitting his pale and scrawny ass down on the edge of the bedspread, his white legs part. I walk to the corner of the room, placing my purse on the small table. Opening the zipper pocket, I pull out one vial of pentobarbital along with a condom.

I turn to him seductively, slowly walking forward with the foil packet in my fingers.

He's grinning excitedly and hardening; I try not to gag. Dropping down to my knees before him, I come face to face with under six inches of scrawny dick. The scratchy carpet rubs against my knees, keeping me on my game.

"Close your eyes," I say in a sing-song voice, a request full of promise. I inch my face forward and hold my breath, exhaling as he shuts his eyes. Without any hesitation, I shoot him in the thigh with the needle.

First comes shock — wide eyes and a mouth open in an "Oh." Anger flashes in his face but before he can act, he drops back onto the bed, disabled.

"Bye motherfucker," I hiss.

I'd punch him, but there's no time. Quickly standing, I grab my bag and focus on getting down to the basement. Opening the bedroom door and looking both ways to make sure no one is around, I count the fourth door to the left from the bathroom, which according to Slade's map, should be the basement entrance.

I open it. There's a long narrow staircase—dark and full of shadows. I move onto the first step, shutting the door behind me and praying there are no cameras trained on me. Then again, nothing about this place is high-tech or organized. I'd say these guys are sloppy, especially on a night like tonight when there's a party going. I shiver as I walk. Nothing but dead silence surrounds me.

What if someone other than Vincent is down here? There could be another man. What if one of the bikers is hanging around? Fear tries to grip me, but I tell it to shut up. Reopening my purse, I take out my loaded gun.

I scurry my way down the steps until I reach the bottom. Light is pouring out from beneath another door. I wrench it open with one hand, my gun lifted high in the other.

The heavy stench of grime and rot coats the air and my stomach twists. Shuffling inside and looking left to right, I keep my pistol up in front of me.

Small room. Old walls. White paint, chipped. Scattered garbage. A random red and silver Nike sneaker alongside an empty Domino's box. Moving forward, my eyes dart around as I kick trash out of my way. Another door. I open it.

It's a small dark room. My eyes adjust. The first thing I see is something large, crumbled on the floor. The smell in here is burned copper. Is it blood? Silence is everywhere.

"Vincent?" I run forward, dropping to my knees. My heart stutters. He's lying in a fetal position. I touch his skin; it's clammy and cold. There are chains behind him, but thankfully, he isn't locked up.

His body is unmoving. I bring my hands to his back. "Baby?" My fingers move to my mouth as I stifle a cry. "Vincent...Vincent." I whisper his name.

Is he dead? I gently push his blood-matted hair away from his face. I must be in shock. My mind isn't fully comprehending this scene. On instinct, I touch his chest. I can feel a slow and ragged breath—it's barely there.

Hours ago, I was sitting at an Italian restaurant with Angelo. And now I am in the basement of a motorcycle clubhouse rescuing Vincent, who could die. It's as though I'm an outsider looking in—there is no more logic to the storyline of my life.

Pulling out my phone, I turn on the flashlight and shine it directly on his face. There's a gash from his eye down to his lip, still oozing.

"What did they do to you?" His eyes are closed. I wish they'd open.

Looking down to his hands, there's just so much blood. His pinky is gone and bone protrudes. I gasp, unable to find a single word to explain this feeling. I want to throw my arms around him and scream —rally against fate, destiny, whatever!

Still, he's alive.

I gather myself, knowing it's time for action.

"Don't worry, baby. I'm getting you out of here." I kiss his bloodied head before lifting my phone.

Me: Basement. It's bad. With Vincent.
Slade: Find door now. I'm west.

I shut my eyes for a brief second, refocusing. It must be on the other end of where I am.

I stand up and run forward, leaving Vincent behind. Pulling open a door, I find a closet—full of guns and ammunition. Their arsenal. And left wide open? *God.* I turn my head around, sweat beading on my forehead. Sloppy or not, these men are dangerous and armed.

"Where the hell is the door? How much time do I have before they come back down? What if Crow wakes up? I should have shot him twice...fuck!"

Another door. I open it. Fresh night air pours in along with Slade.

"Follow me." I'm on autopilot. The door slams shut behind us with a *clang*.

We're back to Vincent. Slade drops to his haunches, deadlifting my life in his strong arms. We walk outside and straight into his black truck, where Vincent's head is placed on my lap in the back seat. I barely notice that Janelle is in the front. She speaks, but I can't hear her.

"I'm here, now," I tell Vincent, my tears dripping from my eyes onto his face. If I were in a fairytale, my tears, full of love and heartbreak, would shatter the spell. The water would drip from my eyes and onto his face and just like that, he'd be brought back to life. But this isn't a fairytale. This is life in all its grittiness.

"Vincent," I start, my voice croaking. "I'm so sorry for leaving. I love you so much," I hiccup, leaning forward and kissing his bloody head. "I can't believe you were unarmed," I quietly wale, remembering being happy at the fact he wasn't carrying. How stupid was I? "I'm never leaving you again. Ever. Please stay with me. Please, baby."

He hasn't budged—not once.

I keep his hand on my bare thigh. For a moment I think he's moving, but I realize his body is only shaking with the car's movements. I pull him closer to me.

We get to the hospital and it all moves in a rush. Vincent is taken away and I collapse into Janelle's arms, the stress finally engulfing me.

"He's safe now, Eve. He'll be all right. You did it." Her soft arms keep me from falling. "Slade's with you now. I'm gonna call a cab to take me back to the plane, okay? I'll be back when I can." She kisses my head before squeezing my hand three times and hands me off to Slade, crying her own tears.

I burst into sobs as we make our way into the stark-white waiting room; the bright lights make me dizzy. Slade brings my small body close to him. I'm so cold. He nestles me tighter. At one point, I look up into his eyes. He's so hard and complicated, but there's something incredibly good about him, too. He's so solid from the outside in. If I ever had a brother, it would have been nice to have one like this.

Hours pass. My heart feels like it's leaking. I finally notice Slade's clothes are bloodied. Mine are, too. Vincent's blood. *Oh God.* Slade tells me to wait a minute. He leaves me alone in the waiting room and returns with two sweatshirts, presumably from the gift shop, and hands one to me. Sliding it over my body, I shiver.

A nurse shuffles out in a white uniform, asking for the family of Vincent Smith. Slade immediately gets up. I'm too dazed to ask any questions about Vincent's alternate name. My anxiety of what will come of Vincent has me close to incapacitated, but I lean on Slade's strength to pull me forward.

The nurse takes us into a small and quiet waiting room when a doctor enters; he looks sixteen, give or take a few years. Is this a joke? Vincent's life is in the hands of a... teenager? I blink hard, trying to cool myself down. Slade's warm hand grabs mine in solidarity.

"Who are you two?" the doctor asks, staring us down condescend-ingly as if he were the adult and we're bad kids in need of punishment.

My annoyance at this child-doctor has me vibrating. "Vincent is my brother," I reply full of attitude, crossing my arms in front of my chest defensively. I will kick this kid's ass! He stares at me skeptically, eyes zeroing in on my outfit. I look down at myself, noticing that I'm not in one of my tailored suits. I look like a hooker in a man's sweat-shirt. But so what? He should be giving me information, not judging me. I fume. What a fucking asshole! The heat of indignation continues to rise as Slade pulls me backward, slightly behind him.

"We appreciate you helping Vincent, doctor. Can you tell us his status?" Slade's voice is all business—exactly what we need. I exhale, letting him take the reins.

"Either of you care to tell me why your *brother* is sliced up like a Thanksgiving turkey?"

"We just found him like that," Slade shrugs a shoulder, his huge muscles bunching beneath his shirt. He's got black circles under his eyes and dark scruff lining his jaw. He looks highly threatening. I cringe, realizing that our current state coupled with Vincent's situation doesn't bode well. I'm sure the cops will come to investigate this eventually. I look up at the doctor as laughter starts to bubble up again in my throat. It's all just too much. Slade gives my hand a squeeze which says: 'you better not fucking laugh right now.' I swallow it down obediently and drop my head to the white-tiled floor.

"Well," the doctor starts, lifting up his blue pen and clicking it twice. "Your brother's pinky is severed. He has a deep knife wound down his face. His cheekbone is broken..."

I stare at the doctor blankly. The entire scenario feels surreal. I can hear the words leaving his mouth, but nothing sinks in.

"...we've put him on serious antibiotics to cure infections—knives can be extremely dirty. He's also got broken ribs, a shattered kneecap, and of course, there's the severe head trauma..."

I step closer, trying to hear better—for some reason, his words sound muffled.

"...we've put him in a coma in order to decrease the intracranial pressure."

I blink. Slade clears his throat. "And how long do you think it will be until you can remove him from the coma?" His dark brows furrowed together. "You will remove him, right?"

"Well, that all depends. I'll monitor the numbers and when it's safe, I'll turn off the sedation."

I find a large white circular clock on the wall. It's five minutes after four in the morning.

"A-are we talking hours? Days? Months?" Desperation has my voice cracking. The doctor may be a kid, but right now, he's all I've got.

"You never really know." He shrugs his shoulders sadly. "Hopefully it won't be more than a few days."

Slade and I turn to each other again before looking back at the doctor. "C-can we go see him?" I cower, embarrassment finally hitting me over my indecent state of dress. The sweatshirt hits my legs in such a way that it looks like I'm not wearing pants.

"Sure," the doctor replies. "He's in 304."

"Is he in any pain?" My voice comes out crackled with intense emotion as I wrap my arms around my middle.

"No. He's not." His voice is decisive.

Slade and I take the elevator to the third floor. The hallway is cold, white, and completely sterile.

We walk into the room. The man in the bed can't be Vincent. It just can't be. His head is bandaged. I can hear the heart monitor beeping. He's technically alive, but he's... gone.

26

EVE

Three Days Later

"Eve?" Lauren walks into the hospital room wearing tight denim jeans and a sexy, off-the-shoulder black T-shirt. A jumbo black Chanel purse is slung over a small shoulder as she pulls a black carry-on suitcase with a small duffle on top behind her. Parking everything in the room's corner by the window, I realize she's here—for me, and I burst into a set of fresh tears.

She quickly moves to me and bends down, hugging me to her chest. "Babe, we gotta get you out of here. Showered. Changed. And food." She's whispering, as though she's afraid to bother Vincent. I'd tell her that he won't wake up no matter what, but the words won't leave my lips. It's too painful.

"N-no." I shake my head. "I c-can't leave him."

"Yes, you can." Pulling out a tissue from the small white cardboard box by Vincent's bed, she hands one to me.

"How did you know to come here?" I sniffle.

"Janelle called—all shady, telling me not to let anyone know I was coming. She was so worried about you." She places a hand on my back. Janelle and Lauren have never met, but after the hundredth time of calling my office and speaking to Lauren, they developed an easy friendship.

She takes stock of my outfit and grimaces. I'm wearing a pair of black leggings, a loose yellow T-shirt, and a pair of black rubber flip-flops courtesy of Slade. After refusing to leave Vincent's side, he stopped at Target and grabbed these clothes and even a toothbrush and face wash for me. Two days ago, the clothes were clean and I was physically back to a semi-normal state. Now, not so much. Adding insult to injury, I have leftover mascara under my eyes that won't come off.

"I went to your apartment and picked up what you need." She points to the rolling suitcase.

"Thank you," my voice shakes. "I don't even—" I pause, feeling an incredible amount of guilt. Lauren is better to me than I deserve. We've worked together for so long and I never gave her enough credit. Never let her into my life the way she deserved.

"Shh," she rubs my back. "Let me pull out clean clothes so you don't have to leave here looking disheveled." Unzipping the bag, she removes a pair of soft navy sweatpants, a fresh nude bra and underwear, and a white cotton T-shirt.

"What did Janelle tell you?" I clutch the clothes to my chest.

"Just that you and Vincent have a long past and he is seriously hurt in the hospital. Also, that you're desperate for clothes and a shower." She stares at my outfit and rumpled, disheveled appearance.

"A-are you mad I didn't tell you about him?" I swallow hard, my mouth feeling dry. I really don't want her to be angry with me.

"Don't tell me you're about to cry again? Ohmygod!" She shakes her head and rubs the beautiful solitaire diamond necklace she always wears around her neck. "Eve doesn't cry. Eve is strong and makes shit happen. A true girl boss. And to answer you, no, I'm not mad. I know how weird it must have been having him as a client. And all you were dealing with, making sure none of the DBC wouldn't catch on. I mean, if they knew about the two of you, they would have pounced. They're disgusting."

Her understanding has me breaking down in another round of tears. We joked about the way they treated me, but both of us knew that none of it was actually funny.

"I was horrible in that office," I mutter, hiccupping. "I'm so sorry—"

"Oh, please," she waves a manicured hand in front of her face. "There was no other way to be. It was like a sanctioned cage fight. Now, go to the bathroom and clean up so we can get out of here for a little while and you can get some fresh air."

I have such a good friend in her. Still, I don't think I'm ready to leave Vincent's side. "I'm afraid to leave him alone. What if he needs me?"

She looks at him sadly. "He's under for now. The best thing you can do is take care of yourself. If you don't, you won't be well enough to care for him when he comes out of this."

I haven't showered or eaten in days and the truth is, I feel on the verge of collapse.

"Okay. Not for long, though." My voice is full of hesitation.

She tucks a long blonde hair behind her ear. "By the way, Jonathan is freaking out. His biggest client is quiet for days, and then you email him about a leave of absence yesterday?" She blows out a puff of air. "I didn't tell him anything, though. Janelle swore me to silence."

"Jonathan can go screw himself." I feel a combination of anger and anxiety. This morning I let him know via email that I had a family emergency and wouldn't know how long I'd need. He replied, but I didn't read it. "This leave will likely turn into my quitting."

Lauren's eyes pop open in surprise before settling in understanding. "Honestly, I don't blame you. You've been dealing with way more than you should. All that harassment. It's seriously out of control the way they treat you in that godforsaken place. You'd think it was still

1987." She shakes her head. "By the way, I emailed the Kids Learning Club for you before I got on the flight over."

"Oh shit, I totally forgot." Guilt crashes through me that I didn't contact them right away.

"Don't worry." She rubs my arm. "They've got people filling in for you. Right now, it's just about the hottie in the hospital bed." She winks and I have to consciously stop myself from laughing out loud.

Lauren takes a chocolate brownie protein bar from her purse and opens the foil wrapper before handing it to me. I slowly bring it to my mouth. Taking a bite, my stomach clenches. Nausea follows.

I must make a face because she pulls the bar from my hand. "You'll have to eat slowly. Actually, why don't you clean up first?"

I swallow, wondering how I manage to eat this garbage every morning. If I never ate another protein bar again, it wouldn't be soon enough. Moving to Vincent, I bend my head to his left hand, kissing each of his fingers slowly, one at a time.

"I'll be back soon, okay baby?" I press his warm palm against my forehead before gently placing it back to his side.

Making my way to the bathroom, I take off my dirty clothes and rinse my face and hands with soap and water. Sliding on my own fresh things, a horrible thought crosses my mind: Does changing mean I'm moving on or giving up on him? "No," I tell myself out loud. "I'm only cleaning up. I'll be back—soon."

"Let's go, honey," Lauren calls, hurrying me. On shaky legs, I step out of the bathroom and into the hallway. Two huge guys sitting in chairs by the door notice me and stand at attention. I suck in a breath of air, scared shitless that these guys are from the BB. *Did they find me?*

"Hey Eve," the bigger one starts gently, raising his arms as if surrendering. His navy spandex T-shirt highlights his muscles. "I'm Cole, and this is Ax. We're friends of Slade." With their military haircuts and serious demeanors, they've got armed forces written all over them. "Ax will accompany you wherever you need to go."

We all look up to see Slade marching down the wide hallway toward us. His back is straight, gait quick, and he walks with purpose.

"Hello," he turns to Lauren, faltering for a moment as he takes her hand in a friendly shake. "Slade," he introduces himself, a redness creeping up his neck. "Janelle told me she asked you to come out." He gives her a genuine smile.

Her jaw slackens. "Y-yeah. No problem," she stutters. "I love you. I mean—Eve. I love Eve!" She lets out a nervous giggle and I bite my cheek.

"Good friends are important," he replies calmly, ignoring her slip.

"Eve, let's talk a second before you go." Slade moves back into Vincent's room, waiting for me to follow.

The moment I re-enter, I can't help but look again at Vincent's still body. My chest constricts.

"Eve," he states, bringing my attention back to him. "A lot has happened in the last few days. I didn't want to bombard you so soon, but now that you're leaving the hospital, you need to know."

"Um, okay," I reply nervously.

"Antonio found out that Vincent escaped the Boss Brotherhood alive. According to Tom, the moment Antonio heard, he ran out of New York City like a bat outta hell. Went rogue. The entire Borignone mafia is on hold right now—no one's sure what's going on."

My hands fly up to cover my mouth.

"Crow was shot in the head yesterday."

"What?" I exclaim in shock.

"Yes," Slade moves his hands to his narrow waist. "It was Antonio, angry that Crow didn't complete the job. He's out for blood. And at this point, it's no secret he blames you for Vincent leaving the family, and apparently, for everything else that's gone wrong."

My heart pounds so hard, I can feel it in my throat.

"Be thrilled that Crow is dead. Otherwise we would have had to worry about him finding out who you are or potentially coming after you."

"Well, what about the rest of the BB?"

"Vincent was only a job to them. Their main focus right now is most likely avenging Crow's death."

I want to feel relieved, but Antonio is the bigger threat. "D-does Antonio know Vincent is here? In this hospital?" My voice shakes.

"Well, I don't know just yet, which is why I want you protected." He presses his mouth together tightly. "You've been so attached to Vincent, you never left to notice I've had his roomed guarded all this time."

I need to take a moment to think. Everything happened too quickly. I never took a second to consider anything other than Vincent. There will be massive repercussions. What kind of backlash could fall on me, or even Janelle back in New York? These gangs are known to intimidate family.

He points to the door. "I've got one of my boys staying here to watch over Vincent and another to be with you, wherever you go. There's a third, his name's Gavin. He'll be doing hospital nightshifts."

"Okay," I reply, my voice small. "Can you arrange a guard for Janelle, too?" I bite my bottom lip. If he says no, I'm sure there's a bodyguard service I can call.

"I've already taken care of that. She'll have Jose by this evening."

"Does she know about it?" I raise my eyebrows nervously. I know the next time I speak with her, I'm going to get hell.

"Yes, I called her yesterday." He tries not to laugh. "That sister of yours is something else." He smirks. "She chewed me out."

"Oh, God." I raise my face to the ceiling. "Are you okay?"

He chuckles. "Don't worry about me, Eve. I can handle her."

"So, she agreed to the bodyguard?"

"Yes. Eventually, she did."

He reaches into his pocket, pulling out a set of keys. "This is for his trailer so you can stay there. I'll text you the address." Nervously, I take them from his hands; the keychain is cold in my palm. I lift it, noticing a small silver boot dangling off the ring.

"Slade, what's this?" My voice catches in my throat as I stare at the charm.

"Oh," his voice is casual, "Vincent picked that up back in New York. He told me he gave the original one away before leaving for prison. When he got out, he bought an identical one for himself."

He gave it to me. It wasn't an accident. Vincent must have wanted me to know that he'd follow me anywhere. And...he did. He came back. But now, he's gone. I can feel the room start to spin.

"Whoa, whoa." Slade pulls me toward him before gently lowering me into a chair. He sits on his haunches in front of me so we're eye level, keeping his hands on my arms to steady me. A terrible thought runs through my head.

"He'll come out of this, Eve," he says, reading my mind. "It's time to be brave. I know you're beat up, but you can't give in to that feeling."

I look directly at him, wanting to agree. But I don't. If Vincent doesn't make it through, I don't think I can go on.

Once I'm steady, Slade helps me to stand and passes me off to Lauren, who links a skinny arm in mine.

"Ax is going to accompany you ladies." Slade keeps his face passive.

"Okay," she smiles wide, "nice to meet you." Waving, Lauren gives him her best cool and calm goodbye.

"Slade got me a hotel room for the night," she whispers conspiratorially as we walk toward the hospital exit. "You think maybe he'll join me if I'm feeling lonely?" She raises her eyebrows and giggles, but I don't reply.

"I think it's where you stayed when you originally came over. Was it nice?" She's trying hard to be friendly and lighthearted. I want to scream at her—tell her that right now isn't the time to be fucking chipper. But I collect myself, knowing my exhaustion and sadness are talking.

"It's beautiful." My voice is machine-like, without intonation. With every step, I feel farther away from Vincent; the distance making my anxiety rise. I should go back to him. I don't want to leave.

"You know what?" I start, my mind officially changed.

She stops walking and faces me. "No," she shakes her head. "You aren't backing out. A shower and a hot meal will do you good. No one is telling you to leave his side. Just take a little break, okay? Plus, think of my life. Janelle will kill me if I don't take you out of here."

Before I know it, Ax is helping us inside the large black Escalade. I'm silent as the driver brings us to the hotel. Lauren, God bless her, is her usual talkative self, keeping him occupied.

I stare out the window, picturing Vincent and me on his bike. Gripping his back while the wind blows over us. The warmth in his eyes when we're in bed. They lighten when he's happy but turn near black when he's emotional.

The car stops in front of the hotel, shaking me out of my daydream.

After a steaming shower, a few bites of a vegetable omelet via room service, and Lauren insisting on blow-drying my hair—two hours have passed. I'm clean, but my emotions feel like roadkill.

We set ourselves up by the wood fire pit on the small terrace. I promised Lauren I'd spend three full hours away from the hospital to revive. The entire setting is the epitome of calm and relaxing, but my heart won't settle. I'm staring at the orange flames as Lauren sips a glass of cold wine from the minibar, likely scanning her social media pages.

She sits forward, putting her empty glass down by the fire. "Okay. Talk to me."

I tell her the whole story. She cries along with me, insisting that love will conquer all. It's exactly the type of thing I'd expect Lauren to say, and I love her for it.

We turn quiet as I stare at the darkness. The mountains, so monstrous in size, can no longer be seen. The night is jet-black with nothing but stars pebbling the sky. I wish I had never left Vincent's side after The Blue. If I only said yes to him right away. I touch my chest, my heart actually squeezing as tears refill my eyes. *I can't lose him.*

And oh, *God*, this shit with Antonio. It took a few hours, but Slade's warnings finally sink in. I stand up and move inside the room, opening my purse. My gun is still here. I clutch it in my hands the same way I did all those years ago in the Blue Houses. But this time, I'm not afraid to use it.

My phone rings and I jump from the sound. I slide the gun back into the bag before taking out my cell. It's Janelle on FaceTime.

I click ACCEPT, and Janelle's face pops up in the center of my screen, blonde hair in perfectly messy waves, face crazy angry.

"Holy fuck, Eve!" Her free hand flies up in the air. "I want you to know how pissed off I am that you haven't called me in three days." Her teeth clench.

"You spoke to Slade though, right?" I know he already told her I'm just fine. And right now, I don't have it in me to argue.

"Yeah, I did." Her reply is both grudging and sad. "Is Lauren with you, now?"

"Yeah, she got to the hospital a few hours ago and brought clothes and forced me to come shower. Thanks for having her come, by the way. And for everything, Janelle. I owe you." I turn my head, seeing Lauren with her head bowed reading on her phone.

"Lauren is seriously the shit," Janelle states. "I'm glad she was able to come. Anyway, move your phone up and down. I want to make sure you're still in one piece."

"Oh, come on—" I nag.

"Just do it. Make your momma happy."

I roll my eyes before moving the phone so she can see my toes up to my face. "Happy now, Granny?"

"I said *momma*, not granny, you bitch." She chuckles and a small snort escapes my mouth.

"As you know, I'm back and alive and fine and Vincent's—" My voice cuts off. I can't say it. I gasp, tears taking the place of words.

Her mouth turns down. "I know. You love him. Just relax. He's...he's going to be okay."

While her words are hopeful, I know she has doubt. In the world we grew up in, life isn't just given and expected to continue until you're old. People die—all the time. Vincent dying young, especially considering the life he used to lead, shouldn't be a surprise.

"I don't know, Janelle."

I wish I could, but I can't escape her pitiful gaze.

"And what about Antonio?" Her voice is gentle. "If you ask me, he's the bigger issue and the looming threat. I've got Mr. Beef watching TV right now in my living room and eating Chinese take-out. Tell me you got a plan?"

"Plan?" I ask her, confused.

"You've seen a million *Law and Order* episodes. Can't you like, go after the bad guy and put him in jail for life? You're the hot blonde lawyer, but obviously, with dark hair." She looks at me as if putting Antonio behind bars is the simplest thing in the world. "He probably has a laundry list of bad shit he's done that the feds can't catch, right?"

"I can help you!" Lauren excitedly screams into my ear. I shudder from surprise; the girl obviously has ninja powers because I didn't even realize she was next to me.

I lick my lips, brain turning. "I don't know, Janelle," I say to the screen. "Let's see."

Lauren brings her face to the camera. "Whenever Eve says 'let's see,' what she really means is, 'I'm doing it!'"

* * *

I put my hand in Vincent's hair, brushing back the dark strands as my nails graze against his scalp; I know he loves when I do this.

"Vincent," I whisper into his ear. "I want to quit the firm. Because I hate it. You were right. They treat me horribly. And I took it all because I thought there wasn't a choice. But there is a choice, and I'm making it now." My hands move to my neck. I rub his cross between my fingers.

Standing up, I pull out a small, portable MacBook. Opening the screen on Vincent's bedside table, I begin typing my resignation.

Once I start, the words flow. I detail the harassment and intolerable work conditions I endured as an associate at the prestigious firm. I'm not looking for any kind of monetary compensation. Instead, I want to specifically pinpoint the failed options for reporting, explaining that I was scared to be punished and therefore stayed silent. My hope is for other women never to have to undergo this abuse.

Draft after draft gets written until I click SEND. It's after two o'clock. I pass out in the wooden chair beside Vincent, holding his hand in mine.

The following morning, I'm leaning my head on Vincent's chest when Lauren walks inside the hospital room carrying two hot coffees in a tray along with a white paper bag.

"You know I'd never touch these sugary carbs. But I figured, if not now, when?" She puts the coffees down on the small side table before handing me the bag full of breakfast desserts.

I sit up to peek inside: croissants and blueberry muffins. "Let me wash up quickly."

"Hurry so your coffee doesn't get cold."

I make my way into the small en-suite bathroom and try to avoid the mirror.

"Lauren?" I ask, walking back toward her. "Would you be able to put up my apartment for sale and maybe hire movers to bring all my clothes out here?" Maybe it's presumptuous of me. Still, where Vincent is, is where I want to be. I have faith he's going to come out of this. And when he does, I need to be here.

"Of course, I can. Did you already resign?" Her eyes are wide.

"Last night." Surprisingly, admitting that I resigned doesn't cause the earth to shatter.

"Harassment is real and shouldn't be tolerated. I hope your letter goes all the way to the top."

"Me too." I press my lips together firmly, nodding in absolute agreement.

Twenty minutes later, she stands to leave. After lots of hugging, one of Slade's guys steps in, letting her know that he'll be escorting her to the airport. With a wink, she leaves my side for California.

I know Slade's army is probably sitting outside, but I pretend they aren't. Reopening my computer, I brainstorm ways to take down Antonio Borignone. I'm not ready to commit to this plan, but a little thinking couldn't hurt. Before I know it, I'm completely in the zone, mapping out ideas.

My phone *pings*, shaking me out of my trance.

Lauren: Eve, it's 9pm. Have you left the room to eat?
Me: okay, okay.

Janelle's name pops up on the screen and I groan. I hate group texts.

Janelle: Go now!
Me: I'm leaving! Je-sus!
Janelle: LOLLLL. Now go.
Lauren: By the way, Janelle, should I use coconut oil on my scalp or will it make it too greasy?

I shut my phone. Maybe I should just sleep on the chair again. But, my back feels like hell and I know that Vincent would rather me stay in a bed. And plus, it'll be HIS bed, so maybe it won't be so bad.

* * *

I enter Vincent's trailer with Ax behind me, who's holding my stuff. I open Vincent's fridge and offer him a cold bottle of water or a beer. Luckily, he declines both and tells me he's going to hang out in his truck to make a few calls and sleep. I already noticed that the back of his pickup was set up as a bed. He walks out and I shut the door behind him, relieved. Not that he isn't a super nice guy, because he is, but I want privacy.

I hesitate at the doorway in front of Vincent's room, slowly taking off my socks and sneakers before finally entering. Pulling a white undershirt from the drawer by his bedside, I slide it on, drowning in worn-in softness. His scent is everywhere, and I'm immediately brought back to last week.

Vincent jumps out of bed, picking me up in his huge arms and carrying me into the bathroom, my entire body feeling completely satisfied after last night. "Vincent put me down, I want to brush my teeth!" I giggle, heart soaring.

Last night. I can't even think the words without flushing. Vincent made love to me as if the world was ending. He's so commanding and dominant. Completely thorough. I'm sure that not one inch of my body was left untouched by his worshipful mouth. He sucked, licked, and kissed every piece of me. And when I thought he was done? He simply gave me more.

Holding me up with one arm, he puts toothpaste on two brushes. I start to brush my teeth, still securely nestled in his chest. I can tell he loves watching me do these random mundane things. His lips move to my neck, as though this simple task is too much for him.

"How am I going to spit like this?" My mouth is full of suds. He grunts, finally lowering me down. I rinse my mouth with water a few times. After drying my face with a small white towel, he lifts me up piggyback style. I press my minty lips against his shoulder as he starts brushing his own teeth.

Glancing in the mirror, my hair is an absolute mess and for the first time in maybe ever, I love it. Our eyes lock. I love this man to no end.

"Your body, Vincent. I still can't believe how much bigger you've gotten." I swallow hard, staring in the mirror at his gorgeous wide chest, down to his six-pack of muscles. "And tan. You're just..." I stop talking, suddenly overwhelmed.

"You didn't notice last night?" He bends his head down to spit in the sink.

"I mean, I did. But..." I can feel a blush creeping into my face. He laughs at me, bringing more water to his mouth while I cling onto him like a little monkey.

Back in the bed, Vincent holds me tightly in his arms; I can barely move a muscle, not that I'd want to. We're not simply embracing—we're fusing.

"I'm keeping this shirt," I speak into his neck.

He pulls away and I watch the smile move through his face and settling in his eyes. "Everything that's mine is yours." He rubs his nose against mine.

"You told me that once before," I remind him. Swallowing, I stare into his deep and dark eyes. It's love.

"And it's still true. Always will be." He pushes a stray hair off my fore-head. I'm home.

I blink and the memory disappears, leaving me all alone in his trailer. My mouth opens wide as tears stream down my face; it's an ugly and painful cry. I manage to fall asleep a few hours later with his pillow over my face, inhaling his smell and praying he'll come back to me.

27

EVE

The next morning, I awake to a knock on the trailer door. I shuffle out of bed, his shirt like a long dress reaching the center of my calves. I move my hands to rub the sleep from my eyes but wince; they're raw.

I peek through the window shade before opening the door.

"Hey, Ax."

The sun shines over the mountains, casting a reddish-orange glow all around. It's so beautiful, but still, I feel a deep sense of sadness. I need to get back to the hospital. I raise a hand like a visor on my forehead, trying to shield my face from the brightness of the sun.

"Sorry to wake you, but I can't leave without your knowledge. I'm gonna run to the store for a very quick errand. Need anything?" He leans against the doorway, a black leather jacket in his hands.

"Nah," I reply. "I want to head back to the hospital in about thirty minutes, though. Think you can drive me over?"

"Yup. Should be back in fifteen." He turns to go, but stops, looking back at me. "Just so you know, Slade installed cameras around the outside of the trailer. I just let him know that I'm heading out for a few, so he'll be watching." Walking to his pickup, he drives away, sand kicking up at the huge wheels as he takes off.

My skin prickles. I look left and right nervously, not noticing anything out of the ordinary. All this shit with Antonio is obviously affecting me. Shutting and turning the lock, I put on a pot of coffee before getting into the shower. Instead of using the shampoo and conditioner Vincent and I picked up together, I use his Dove Men's shampoo and body wash, wanting to smell like him. In some strange way, it makes me feel closer. I step out of the shower and put on a comfortable pair of relaxed-fit jeans and a white T-shirt, texting Ax I'm ready to go.

I hear a noise. Someone else is here. My breath stops as I listen intently.

Bending down, I grab the gun from my purse. Water drips from the ends of my dark hair, soaking the back of my white T-shirt. The silence is eerie, but my instincts are on high.

I step to the bedroom door and stare through the sliver of an opening. My eyes focus on a familiar man with salt and pepper hair, sitting at Vincent's small and round kitchen table. I keep watching as he slowly turns his head, licking his full lips like a wolf.

A sneer is settled on his chiseled and cruel face; I'm taken aback. He looks so much like Vincent, it's staggering. But those eyes, a cold electric blue, are vacant.

Antonio Borignone.

"I know you're watching me, Eve," he says loudly, body turned toward the bedroom door. "Come out," he says in a sing-song voice.

My heart slows as I realize there is nowhere to go. I consider jumping out the bedroom window, but there is no way I can fit through. I briefly consider hiding, but if he already knows I'm here, he'll surely come and find me. I've got to strengthen myself and move forward. Ax will walk in any minute now—I just need to stall. Tucking the gun in the back of my pants, I take a tentative step out of the room.

"The girl who shook my empire." He starts a slow clap as I walk closer to where he sits. "Sit," he commands. My heart beats straight into my throat.

I take a seat, doing my best not to show any emotion or weakness. I know from Vincent there's no quicker way to get myself killed.

"Look at you." His voice is unnervingly calm as he stares me up and down, considering what's before him. Pulling a cigarette from a Marlboro Red pack at the center of the table, he lights up and takes a deep inhale.

I remember the first time I met him at Angelo's pawnshop; he's still just as frighteningly magnetic. But I'm no longer the scared girl I once was. I straighten my back, waiting to hear what he has to say. If I'm going to die, I won't go down as a scared child. He notices the shift in my demeanor and smiles.

Still, I try to keep my face unreadable.

"The little girl from the hood has risen," he says, seemingly to himself. His fingers tremble as he brings the cigarette back into his mouth for another long drag, the smoke billowing from his mouth as he speaks. "I remember you as a terrified kid. And now here you are —trapping my son with that pussy of yours."

His fist, resting on the table, clenches.

"He went to prison seven years ago." He leans back into the chair and crosses one leg over his knee. "I figured that would be the trick to get you guys separated for good. You see, a woman like you is terrible for business. Love? I hate the word. In the same way I hate all pathetic and needy people." He grinds his teeth, pitching forward. "But could he just forget you? Nope. Vincent comes out of lockup and heads straight here." He lifts his hand like an airplane and flies it toward me. "You fucked up his head, girl."

His eyes are unfocused. He's on a rant, so much in his own mind that I wonder if he even realizes I'm sitting in front of him. Antonio Borignone is no longer the self-contained man I knew. No wonder Vincent thought the family was a losing bet.

"What a joke," he hisses. "To think my son now lives in a fucking trailer on an Indian Reservation. Left the family for this fuckin' shit. And with a woman from the goddamn gutter."

He stands up and walks to the wooden kitchen cabinets, pulling one open. With a sweep of his hand, spices and cans clatter onto the ground and roll around the floor.

"He should be living like a king, running the Milestone while readying himself to run my empire." He laughs, shaking his head as he turns back to me. "He should be the prince I raised him to be. But for you, he gives up his life and all the possibilities and the money and the power and the women. It's sickening."

I glance up at the clock. *Where is Ax?*

"If you're waiting for that moron to come for you, you're wasting your time. I shot him in the head just as he left." He shrugs casually, sitting back down in the chair.

Before I can feel terror, a thought hits me like a freight train: It's not my time. Vincent is going to come out of his coma and when he does, I'm going to be by his side. I'm not letting this lunatic take it all away.

And for maybe the first time in my life, I know I deserve better. All my life, it was about working hard and getting out of the ghetto. But no matter how high I climbed, I never believed I was actually *worth* more. I've been pushed around and bullied for years. My mother's emotional abuse. My near rape with Carlos. Daniela, the bitch from hell. Even Jonathan and the DBC. And now this psycho—who sent his own son to jail and tried to murder him—blames me for Vincent and me falling in love? I'm finished with this shit. I know who I am and I know my value. The days of letting people run over me are done. I shift in my seat, steadying myself. If I go down today, it will not be quietly.

"You have anything to say before you die?" He pulls out his gun and grips it in the palm of his hand. The look in his eyes completely unhinged. A voice inside my head tells me to keep him talking and delay our standoff. If the camera was on like Ax had said, Slade should have seen Antonio entering. Still, if one of us has to die, it won't be me. To make it out alive, I'm ready to do whatever it is I have to do.

"Vincent told me that your uncles started the Borignone mafia."

My voice comes out stronger than it has the right to be. "It's so impressive what you've accomplished. Clearly, you took what they started and created an empire. How did you manage it?"

If my memory from Psychology 101 serves me right, egomaniacs are possessed by delusions of prominence, but frequently feel a lack of appreciation. Hopefully, this should get him talking.

He places the gun down on the table before grazing the muzzle with his index finger. Turning his head toward the window, he stares at the mountains.

"I began as a kid. Let me tell ya, my uncles were the real deal. I met your mother shortly after I started with 'em. She was gorgeous and wild, recently came from Russia with a baby. Danced at one of our clubs. Enzo had a thing for her." He taps the end of the cigarette, ash snowing on the floor. "Threw a vase at one of the doors in your shitty apartment, once." He laughs as if reminiscing about the golden days. My heart slows to a steady pound. *It's working.*

"She used to party with us. Hot as fuck. Into the drugs, of course." He takes another smoke from the pack and lights it up. "Complained a lot about you. That's why she got you the job with Angelo. Figured if you stayed in our hold, you'd keep it in mind who you were and stop dreaming." He blows upward, smoke circling around his head like a devilish halo.

"There are people in this world who eat shit. And because they do, they think that every other person on the planet should, too. They hate anyone who tries to do better because they themselves can't do better. That's your mom. And let me tell ya, she wasn't wrong.

Lifting a finger, he points at my face. "Your mom and I were always on the same page. Sure, I lived like a king and she was addicted to meth. But both of us set our lives in motion. Your mother was a crack whore. Why should you be allowed to just escape or do better? She had no choice but to stay in the life—why should you be able to just leave when she couldn't? And why should Vincent be allowed to just do whatever-the-fuck he wants?" He slams his hand down on the table and his cigarette flies out of his mouth and onto the floor. I don't allow my body to jump.

"I created a kingdom," he shouts, looking at me with crazed eyes. "Vincent doesn't get to just walk away. I'm the creator. I'm the ruler." He pants, his mouth foaming white at the corners.

My hand steadily presses against the gun in the back of my jeans. The man is so involved in his words, he wouldn't notice the entrance of a wild animal. I internally smile.

Life isn't just about escaping my past circumstances but thriving despite them. With confidence I never knew I possessed, I remove the piece, aiming it straight in front of me. I can't stall any longer. Antonio pauses, mouth settling on a smirk. The asshole thinks I don't have the guts.

"You see, Antonio." I lick my dry lips before pointing the gun at the center of his head. "Me and Vincent aren't in your hold anymore. And now there is another thing you and my mother have in common. She's dead. And so are you."

I pull the trigger on the exhale. Blood, black like tar, and pieces of bone and brain matter spray across the room. I'm not sure how long I'm sitting there with the gun clasped in my hands, but the next thing I know, Slade is running into the trailer saying something I can't understand.

He's got me in his arms and I feel warmth and safety. I turn to him as he speaks. "The doctor called—he's waking Vincent up today. Antonio is dead, now. You're free. Do you hear me, Eve? You're free."

"V-Vincent?" I manage to stutter out, shaking.

"Just calm down now. You'll be all right."

I hear an ambulance in the distance as I hang onto Slade, clinging to him as my body trembles in shock.

* * *

Slade accompanies me to Vincent's room, leaving me at the doorway to give us privacy. The nurse shuffles out. "Be gentle, darling. He doesn't remember much of what happened." I make my way inside, slowly.

Vincent turns his head to me and I can't stop my gasp. Dark, red-rimmed eyes. Heavy black scruff along his jaw. Slash down his face, stitched. Hair overgrown.

But, he's here.

"Come." His voice is a dry and broken rasp.

I run toward him and drop my head on his chest, thinner from drugs and ventilation.

"Tell me. What happened?" He asks.

I take a piece of ice with my fingers from a cup on his side table and bring it to his cracked lips. He shuts his eyes in relief as it melts into his mouth. He stares at me again, waiting for me to speak. I drop the cube back into the cup before breaking down and spilling everything. How the B.B. was hired by his father to take him. Entering the clubhouse. Crow. When I get to killing Antonio, his shock and relief are palpable as understanding fills his face.

I grip his hand. "We're free."

"We're free," Vincent repeats my words slowly, as if he needs to come to terms with them, too.

"I've been here since yesterday morning. The tribal police—they had so many questions. I was stuck here, answering everything. I k-killed him. Antonio is dead now. Self-defense, of course. The cameras show him breaking and entering and—"

He hums, shutting his eyes. Seeing Vincent so weak is devastating.

When it's time for discharge, I ask the nurse to leave so I can help him dress. His entire body seems broken and yet, here he is—with me. I know he'll heal.

We get into the car and take the back seat as Slade drives us back to the trailer.

I begin crying into Vincent's shoulder.

"I wake up from a coma to see you constantly crying?" His lips quirk in a small smile, different from his old one—almost, weary. His entire face is so bruised, I can barely recognize him.

I cry harder. "I'm crying because I love you. I'm crying because I'm so happy you're w-with me." I keep my arms wrapped around his chest because I can't let go. If he isn't comfortable, he doesn't say.

"Are you staying tonight?" His words come out insecure.

"I'm figuring out my next steps. Lauren's selling my apartment and I resigned from work. I'm here now."

"We'll work it all out together, yeah? We've got time. But if you want, you can go—"

"No. I'm doing this. I'm going to explore a different path for my life. The firm wasn't working for me and anyway, I have some ideas." He squeezes my hand in his.

I'm emotionally crumbled, but Vincent is with me. It's the best day of my life.

28

Six Months Later

Angelo stands on a flat rock, smiling happily in a black pinstriped suit as beads of sweat drip down his sideburns. In order to officiate this moment, he became ordained. As the only father Eve has ever known, I know it means the world to her that he's doing this. He stares at me in deference and I nod my head back in reply. It's a little piece of my old life.

The mountains surround us, giving us privacy, yet looming large and serving as a reminder that there is something greater out in the universe above us all.

Eve and I hiked here when I was well enough to walk. She made us sandwiches of fresh-baked bread, roasted turkey, and vegetables. Packing it all together with two miniature wine bottles and chocolate chip cookies, she managed a perfect feast. It only took half an hour for her to get tipsy and giggling. My heart got so fuckin' full, there was nothing left to do but get down on a knee and swear my never-ending love and devotion. I would have begged if I had to, but luckily, she only wrapped her arms around my neck and cried.

Lauren and Janelle stand on the left side of Angelo, both in short colorful dresses. Slade and I are situated on his right, wearing khaki slacks and white shirts. Janelle gives me a half smile as if she's saying, "Let's make peace." I chuckle, knowing that beneath that nice-girl façade she's cursing me. She is going to have to learn to deal with me, though. Eve's about to be my wife, and I plan on never letting her out of my sight until the day I die.

Slade taps my shoulder. "Any minute now, brother." He faces ahead and I watch him flush. He's staring at Lauren, who's adjusting the straps on her dress. I've never seen Slade as anything but serious, and truthfully, I like it. Lauren's a good girl.

I was angry at him for risking Eve's life to save mine, but she convinced me to forgive him. Eve made it clear that she is her own woman, and she was the one who chose to come to my rescue. "...I'm not a doll Slade can control. He put out the option, and I took it." I can't stop the smile spreading across my face because Eve is every-thing, and then some. *Damn*, I love my woman.

It took her time to come to terms with the fact that she killed Antonio, and emotionally, she wasn't doing so well. While the feds—down to the local police—knew that she acted out of self-defense, killing a man, no matter how deserved, is a sickening feeling and something I understand all too well.

Returning from the hospital, she began having dreams that she killed me instead of my father. Sweating and crying out, I tried to wake her gently, not wanting to shock her. When she'd come to realize I was still next to her, she would only cry harder.

The last few months, she's been getting much better. With the help of a fantastic psychologist, who she speaks with a few nights a week on video chat, Eve's beginning to cope with everything from her mother's abuse up to killing Antonio. Finally living together without any constraints or secrets helps, too. We cook and work and love each other daily.

My fingers move to my face, the scar from my eye down to my

chin is raised and still slightly tender. The pinky on my right hand is gone, although I do have phantom pain. My limp is here to stay, thanks to my shattered kneecap. While my physical body has taken a serious beating, I'm lucky to say I've still got all my mental faculties. The Milestone is no longer encumbered by any Borignone interference. Life is better than ever.

Tom stepped up as the new boss. He and I spoke. He swore no one will ever touch me again; the entire underground knows that I am no longer affiliated. Turns out one of the newer members had an idea of how the family can clean and house their dirty cash out in Argentina and the Milestone is no longer necessary for their operation. Regardless, I know Tom would never keep me tethered. The family may be my past, but Tom and I will always be brothers.

At any rate, today is not about yesterday. It's about starting my life with the only woman I've ever loved. The photographer I hired comes over to where the five of us stand, taking snapshots to memorialize the moment. The lone violinist, sitting a few feet away from us, plays the instrumental version of "Next to Me" by Imagine Dragons. My heart pounds. This is our song.

I blink and she appears—Eve. A long white gown with delicate straps falling off her slender shoulders, she glides down the small aisle filled with white flower petals. She slightly bends her head to stare at her feet, all innocence and truth. I couldn't stop my own tears if I tried. I already know she's wearing no jewelry. Our mutual commitment is based on who we are as people, not on any material possessions.

I remember her as a kid sitting with me in a pizza shop, eating together and talking about Italy. Teaching her to skate in Central Park while she gripped onto me for dear life. Studying in our bed down in SoHo, buds in her ears as she memorized mathematical formulas beside me. The woman I found her to be when I returned from prison. Brilliant and so beautiful.

And now? My wife.

Solo, she makes her way to the center of the aisle. I feel a pang in my chest—Eve shouldn't walk alone. Not anymore. My feet move on their own accord as I limp into the aisle. She smiles as I reach her, eyes full of joy. Taking her hand, we walk together to where Angelo and our friends stand. Janelle steps forward, handing her a soft white shawl.

"Wrap this around our shoulders," Eve tells me, smiling. "Let it symbolize that we're bound."

I do as she asks, covering us in soft cloth as Angelo begins the ceremony. When it's time, I kiss every finger of her left hand before placing a plain gold ring on her finger. It has no blemishes or stones, serving as a symbol that our marriage will be one of simple beauty. My voice is stronger than ever as I swear to always love and protect her.

After placing an identical ring on my finger, she too swears to always love and protect me. We say the words but both know, deep down, we've already proven our vows to each other. I'm struck by the fact that she's next to *me*. Loving *me*.

Our friends clap as we kiss, cheering. I bend down to press my forehead against Eve's, raising the shawl above our heads and repeating over and over again against her lips how much I love her. It's no one but us.

We all walk to the picnic area of the park where I surprise Eve with a party filled with music, all of her favorite foods, and twinkling lights. I told Kimber how I envisioned the night, and she managed it perfectly. Eve's always had a thing for delicious meals and dancing. Even though she said she didn't need or want a party, she should have it all tonight while surrounded by the people she loves.

"Vincent, how could you?" She slaps my shoulder and I laugh. Her face is warm and utterly euphoric.

"There was no way I was going to let this moment go without celebration." I wrap my arms around her tiny frame, bringing her against me. "Plus, we've gotta dance together, yeah?"

The violinist is joined by a drummer, guitarist, and keyboard player. I hired a DJ as well, because the band couldn't play all the music Eve loves. Janelle wrote out a list of songs for him and I laughed when I saw the lineup. The girls have a serious thing for

Drake that's been going on for years. Slade told a few of his friends to come as well, and they meander over to where we are with beers in hand, clapping me on the back in congratulations.

We're all dancing to OutKast's "Hey Ya!" when Claire and Ms. Levine, Eve's high school English teacher, walk over. Eve's jaw drops in shock as she runs to hug them wholeheartedly.

Eve hasn't seen Ms. Levine in years, but they've kept in touch via email. As the woman who picked up my girl by the bootstraps and got her out of Blue Houses hell, I'm forever indebted. When I called her with the news of our wedding, she was over the moon with happiness.

Claire and Eve haven't seen each other since Columbia, but they've kept in touch for all these years, too. Claire was in Algeria with Doctors Without Borders and it was purely coincidental that she was back in the states for a two-month vacation while our wedding was happening. Seeing her is bittersweet; she was part of the best and the most terrible of times.

As the guests eat and hang out by the bar, Eve and I continue to dance under the evening moon, our own pace nice and slow despite the beat of the music. My hands stay on her at all times. I know I'm greedy, but I just can't let her go.

"Eve?" I bring her closer.

"Mmm?" she hums, smiling.

"You gave yourself to me." She squints in annoyance. I know it drives her insane when I talk macho, but her mad face is just so damn sexy.

"Vincent," she says my name all angry, and I have to stop myself from dragging her out of here and taking her to bed.

"Now that I'm your husband, I'll be more protective. Extra crazy, too. Gonna need you next to me all the damn time." She gives me another face. "Can't help it, babe."

"Is it too late to back out?" My mouth turns down and she giggles, slapping my arm. "Oh, come on. As if I don't know you."

"Well, that's why I think we should build out your center next to my office trailer. This way I can always be near."

"You were able to get the land?" She lets out an adorable squeak.

I nod slowly and her eyes flash in excitement. The last few months, Eve has been planning logistics of her domestic violence shelter. With five short-term residences and a specialization in building life skills, employment assistance, and legal counseling for battered women and their families, she hopes to give families a safe place to restart their lives and rise above their current situations.

Eve went through hell by the hands of her own mother, but with an iron will and the support of her sister and Ms. Levine, she was able to claw up and out. Still, most people aren't so lucky or as strong. This shelter will be a support and savior in the way these families need.

I touch her gorgeous dark hair, down and wild the way I love, and feel immeasurably lucky. "I'll spend my life making myself worth it. I swear." I kiss the top of her head softly before she tilts her head up, giving me those warm, full lips. My entire soul stirs.

"Vincent. Vincent. Vincent," she says my name over and over like a blessing.

"Yeah, baby?"

"We're married." She looks at me then, in a way only Eve ever has. And with every ounce of love within me, I kiss her.

The End

LOVE WHAT YOU JUST READ?

Books in the Vincent and Eve series:
Rising (Vincent and Eve Book 1)
Reckoning (Vincent and Eve Book 3)
Redemption (Vincent and Eve Book 3)

You can check out all of my books on my Amazon author page:

https://amzn.to/2LcsIr7

Want to know about sales, updates, news, and receive bonus content? Sign up for my newsletter:

http://jessicarubenauthor.com/newsletter/

Interested in hanging out with me and chatting all-things bookish? Join my Facebook group, Jessica's Jet Setters:

https://bit.ly/2lHuCaZ

I love to hear from readers! Please reach out to me via my website:

http://www.jessicarubenauthor.com

Readers,

Did you know the Vincent and Eve series was my debut? As a brand-new author who independently publishes, reviews have the power to make or break a book. If you have the time, please drop a line on Amazon or Goodreads! It would truly mean the world to me.

With Love,

Jessica Ruben

ACKNOWLEDGMENTS

This book has been an incredible journey. Without certain individuals, the finish line would never have been reached. Firstly, I need to thank my husband for giving me the space and support I need to follow my dreams. Jon, you're the breath in my prayers. I love you more. I must also thank my children, who make me believe in the purity of human beings. Because of my family, I know that love is truth.

I want to thank my team. First on the list is Leigh Ford, my master Beta reader. When things got stressful, you were the one talking me through my words. Helping to outline and brainstorm. You're the scaffolding for not only these books, but also for life. I also need to thank Andrea at Hot Tree editing, Candice, Caitlin, Jana, Roxy, and Jayme for Beta-reading. Your support in these books gave me the strength I needed to plow forward. Lauren Runow—my big sister in this author world. I adore you. M.J. Fields!! Your support and love for Vincent and Eve along with the friendship you've offered me still feels like a dream come true.

Now here comes the part when I talk about the big gun. Autumn at

Wordsmith Publicity. You are fierce. You are brilliant. And you literally picked my debut books by their straps and threw them, with all your might, onto the map—all with class and determination. You're amazing. I am so thankful to call you my publicist, but even more thankful to call you my friend.

I have to thank Ellie from Love N' Books for reading the earliest draft of my work and encouraging me to split the novel into three. Your guidance and knowledge of the book world is second to none. From small wording changes to large plot issues—I'm lucky to say my books were all in your excellent care.

BilliJoy Carson at Editing Addict. You are so skilled at what you do. You dissect my work like a book surgeon! And your attention to detail are what took my books from "good" to "as good as they could be." I thank you.

The bloggers. You ladies are amazing. You shouted my books from the social media rooftops and brought me to Kindles around the world. You're the gatekeepers of the book community and I admire all of your hard work and dedication. Most of all, I admire your passion for the craft and love of books. I may be a storyteller, but you guys shed the light. I am so grateful you all took a chance on me.

The readers!! Thank you, thank you, THANK YOU for reading. For clicking on an unknown and taking that risk. I hope you enjoyed the journey of Vincent and Eve.

Made in the USA
Middletown, DE
23 September 2018